THE BROKEN LEG AND THE BROKEN P&L

ANJALI VAISHAL

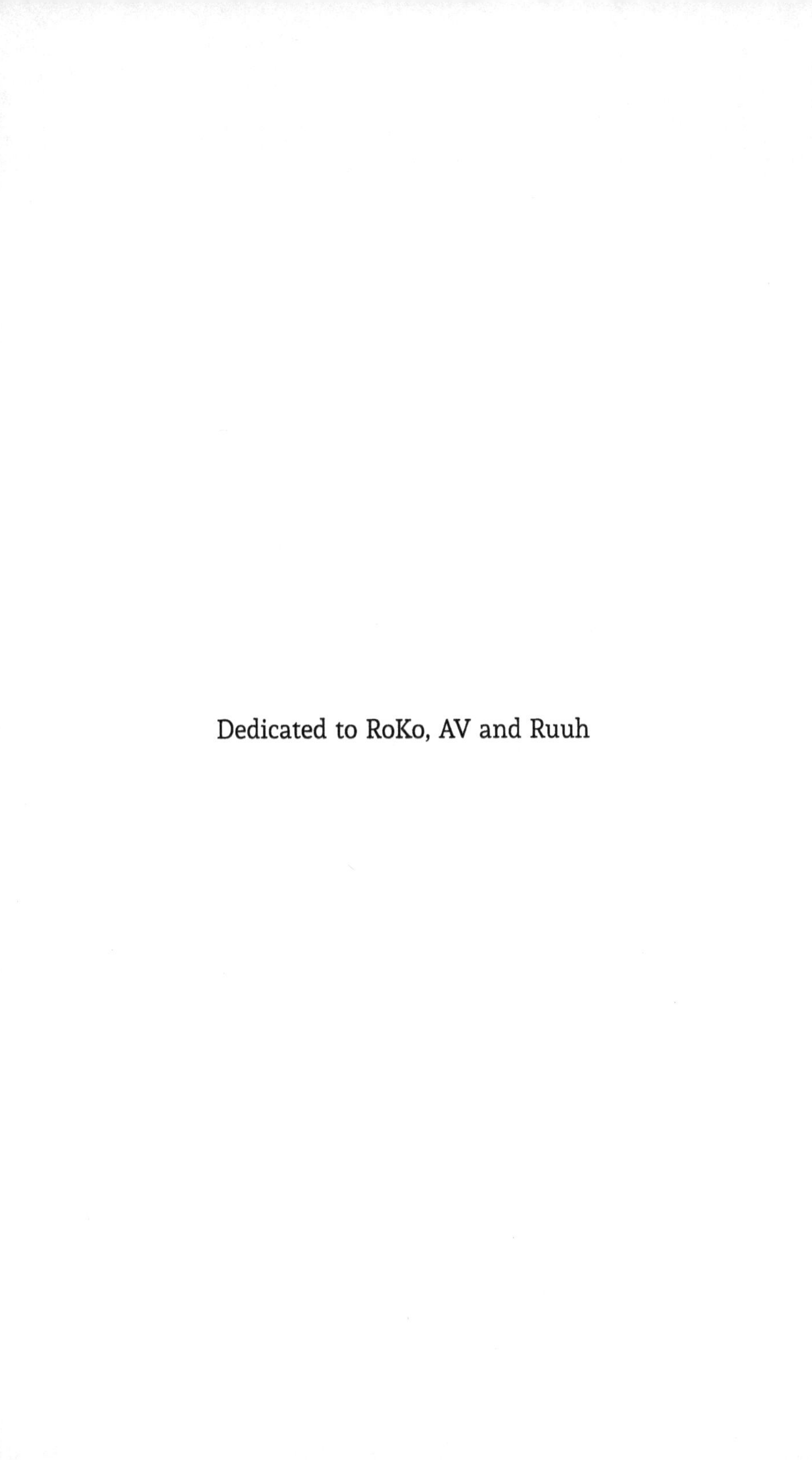

Dedicated to RoKo, AV and Ruuh

Contents

Preface

Every once in a while, a story comes along that isn't just told—it's truly felt. The ones that resonate the most are often the simplest and most honest. *And this is one of those stories—a glimpse into the tangled emotions and fragile connections that make us human.* But don't be tricked by its simplicity; this tale carries unexpected twists that will make you question how well you understand togetherness and how little we control where it leads.

RoKo, a free spirit with an infectious laugh and boundless energy, had a way of lighting up every room she entered, while AV, a quiet thinker with a heart full of untold stories, often found himself drawn to the sidelines, observing. Their worlds couldn't have been more different—one moved fast, lived in the moment, while the other stayed cautious, carefully choosing his path. When their paths crossed, it was as if two different universes collided, their connection immediate, powerful, and full of promise. But with that connection came challenges neither expected.

What started as shared moments and laughter, with nights that stretched into mornings, soon grew more intricate. The differences that once drew them together, now tested their ability to understand each other. RoKo's spontaneity clashed with AV's reserve, leaving both to wonder: Can togetherness thrive between two people so different?

As RoKo encouraged AV to step out of his comfort zone, and AV urged RoKo to slow down and reflect, a deeper connection emerged, peeling back layers of their own souls and discovering truths buried deep. But what happens when two people see sides of each other that even they are afraid to confront? *Eventually, they are forced to decide whether togetherness is enough—or if it's time to walk away.*

In their journey, they soared to incredible heights, where togetherness felt like a limitless force, and plummeted to unimaginable depths, where silence and doubt became their greatest enemies.

There were moments of joy that felt timeless, when the earth seemed to spin faster, and nothing could break what they had built, and those quiet, still moments when doubts whispered just loudly enough to make them question everything, as if time itself had paused.

It wasn't a dramatic event that threatened to tear them apart but the small things—the unspoken fears, the togetherness strained under the weight of unsaid words and unmet expectations.

This isn't the perfect story. There are no tidy endings because life rarely gives us those. Instead, this narrative embodies the real world—a place where missed opportunities hang like shadows, words left unsaid carry more weight than those spoken, and togetherness—no matter how deep—sometimes struggles against the walls we build around ourselves.

As you turn the pages, echoes of your own life might resonate in RoKo and AV's story. Perhaps you'll recognize moments left unsaid, the familiar pang of missed chances, or the bittersweet recognition of togetherness slipping away. Or maybe you'll find hope—the kind that keeps us going, believing that, no matter what, there is always something to cherish and learn from every relationship.

You'll wonder if they'll make it, if they'll overcome the obstacles multiplying with every turn. You'll question if they'll find their way back to each other or if their togetherness was perhaps meant—or never meant—to be.

But through it all, one thing remains constant: the story's ability to captivate, to make you reflect, and to remind you that life, like togetherness, doesn't always give us the endings we wish for.

This isn't just RoKo and AV's story—it's ours too. Step into their world, and you may see reflections of moments we've all lived through in some way.

So let's get the story started :)

Acknowledgements

I feel incredibly lucky to have this chance to thank all the amazing people who have helped shape me into the person I am today. Life's journey is a wild ride, and I've been fortunate enough to have some truly remarkable people right there with me, adding Radiance, Energy, and a whole lot of Spark to the mix.

From my fiercely loving family to my remarkably inspiring friends, each one has fuelled my fire and added a burst of colour to my world. This book is a testament to all those moments—an exhilarating journey we've been on together, whether you realized it or not.

This isn't just a story; it's an explosion of experiences, laughter, lessons, and love, all wrapped up with a powerful punch of Heart and Soul. And let me tell you, this is just the beginning. There are so many more stories waiting to be unleashed, all thanks to the phenomenal people who make my life a thrilling, high-energy expedition.

Here's to all the dynamic relationships that have filled my life with meaning, joy, and a relentless drive to keep pushing forward. You've made this journey not just special, but truly extraordinary.

Being so full of love in the moment and overwhelmed with emotion, the question is, where do I get started? Well, let's start right where it all began.

The collective—this opportunity has shown me the incredible power of the collective. As they say, there are no coincidences in life, and I'm learning to truly believe that. *Some people come into your life for a reason, some for a season, and some for a lifetime.* I've been fortunate to have a rich abundance of these luminous souls and divine energies in my life.

My mom, The strongest person I've known. She's always been my rock, pushing me to get back up quickly after any setback. Her tough love might have been hard at times, but it taught me to be resilient and always aim higher. I owe so much of who I am today to her strength and guidance. Mom your love nourishes my spirit, and your wisdom guides my steps.

My dad for nudging me in the ways he did. Thank you, Papa, you've taught me resilience and integrity, always leading by example. I'm grateful for every lesson and every moment of support.

Sam, He is the wind beneath my wings, the one who ensured I remain collected through every storm. I can't thank him enough in this lifetime; truly, he is the best thing that ever happened to me. His unwavering support and inspiration drive me to reach for the stars and never settle for less, constantly reminding me of what's possible when you have the right person in your corner. The second book came to life solely because of you. Thank you, Sam.

My Mother in law, She has always been my unwavering support, teaching me the true meaning of unconditional love. Her constant smile and boundless positivity are a source of inspiration for me. I'm deeply blessed by the support system she has created, giving me the freedom to pursue my dreams without any conditions. If everyone could be as fortunate as I am, they'd know that you can chase your passions and still have a joyful, proud, and successful family. Thank you, Ma.

My best father-in-law, for the love and affection he has always showered on me. He has always ensured I have everything that I need from the bananas for my gym workout to the dhokla breakfast cravings to the night sugar rush and rasgulla stories, and to top it all the pocket money that I still get from him for all my travels. I couldn't have been blessed more.

My sister and my brother, the nappy babies (I know I would be cursed for a couple of years for saying this out loud) who I wanted to pack in my bag and take them to school every day, they taught me how to be responsible and think beyond oneself and their stories will follow in my upcoming books. **Anku** has been my moral compass, the soul with the purest intentions-even for those least deserving... And then there are those two cute little devils, Kiyan and Kavyan. They gently remind me of my place, time and again, proving that their love and care know no bounds. Their innocent smiles and honest questions keep me grounded and constantly remind me of what truly matters in life.

My sister in law, where only the words in law make no sense, she loved me and loves me so much more, well before her wedding more than herself, after her wedding a little less than Peepo (the sunshine who makes our world brighter), Vaibhav and of course her mother and my North Star.

And last but not least, to everyone who has been a part of my journey-those who supported me with their blessings and affection, some with their presence and others with their absence- Thank you.

Your influence, whether near or far, has shaped me in countless ways. I am deeply grateful for each and every one of you.

Thank you. Thank you. Thank you.

ONE
RAVISHING ROKO

❦

**Singularity Wasn't Her Style, in Multiplicities and Abundance
Did She Thrive and Come Alive...**

RoKo never did things halfway. To say she had a penchant for excess would be an understatement—she reveled in it, wrapped herself in it like one of her beloved Burberry stoles elegant, timeless, and oh so very RoKo. If she liked something, she didn't just indulge; she immersed herself completely.

This extended beyond material possessions; it was a principle that guided her life. For RoKo, one was never enough; two was just the beginning, and sometimes more was simply a necessity.

Take her Onitsuka shoes, for instance. What started as a practical purchase—two pairs to alternate during her long workdays with the intent to keep her feet comfortable—*quickly spiraled into a collection of twelve. Each pair had a purpose, a story, a reason for being, though to the outside world they might have seemed identical.*

To RoKo, they were anything but ordinary. There was the pair she wore for her early morning meetings, the ones she reserved for Friday dressing, and some more for the weekends. Then there were those that were just too pristine for anything other than a leisurely stroll through the city. Each pair carried a memory, a specific purpose—an armor for whatever the day demanded.

In many ways, her shoes weren't just shoes; they were an extension of her identity, markers of the miles she had walked, both literally and figuratively, to get to where she was.

But the comfort they provided wasn't always enough to quiet the memories of her childhood—memories that had shaped her more than she cared to admit. One evening, as she carefully arranged her shoes in perfect order, she was suddenly transported back to being nine years old, staring down at her scuffed, hand-me-down shoes as she walked to school. They had once belonged to her older cousin, and she remembered the sting of envy watching her classmates in their shiny new shoes. In that moment, a quiet determination had taken root in her—she promised herself that one day, she'd never have to wear someone else's cast-offs again.

The memory of those worn-out shoes haunted her, a reminder of the days when she had felt *invisible*, unseen in the shadows of others. Each pair she bought as an adult was a silent defiance against that past, a way to assert her presence in the world, to say, "I am here, I matter."

But sometimes, in the quiet of the night, when she stood in front of her immaculate shoe collection, *the old insecurities would creep back in. Was she really as confident as she projected, or was it all a facade built on layers of leather and laces?*

Her love for business suits was another testament to her philosophy of abundance. RoKo didn't just buy suits; she curated them. Over thirty pieces hung in her wardrobe, each in a different shade, each carefully chosen for the statement it made.

There was the deep navy suit that exuded authority, the soft gray that spoke of quiet confidence, and the bold red that she reserved for days when she needed to command the room—or the Zoom.

Every morning, as she stood before her closet, she didn't just dress for the day—she dressed for the person she needed to be and the role she had to play in her universe.

But sometimes, as she adjusted the lapels of one of her favorite suits, a whisper of doubt would creep in. *Was she truly dressing for herself, or was she armoring herself against the world's judgments?*

She remembered the early days of her career when a senior colleague had once remarked on her *"sharp"* appearance. It was meant as a compliment, but it had felt like a double-edged sword—sharp because she needed to be, to cut through the doubt, the insecurities, the fear of not being enough.

That comment, stayed in her mind like an unanswered question. *It haunted her, replaying over and over, until she questioned every choice she made, every piece of clothing she adorned herself with.*

Dialogue could have helped break this spiral, but RoKo rarely confided these thoughts to anyone. She internalized them, letting them fester, a silent battle that no one else could see.

One evening, after yet another comment about her so-called *"extravagance,"* RoKo found herself on the phone with her mother, reminiscing about their early years. *"You've always wanted more,"* her mother said, not unkindly. *"But remember, sometimes less is more too."* RoKo was silent, the words sinking in deeper than she expected.

She was forced to confront a truth she'd been avoiding: perhaps her desire for more wasn't just about security—it was about proving something to herself, to the world.

She hesitated, then let out a sigh, aware, deep down, that her shopping sprees were less about the items and more about a longing she could never quite satisfy. Yet, she still didn't know how to address that longing, how to fill the void without her usual crutches.

Tumi bags were another indulgence, but to RoKo, they were more than just functional accessories. They were companions on her journey, each one holding memories of airports, hotels, and business meetings that spanned continents.

She owned two of the same model, each in a different shade, because why limit herself to just one when each color carried its own story? *The sleek olive-green fauji backpack was for business trips*—professional, no-nonsense, a bag that got the job done. It had been with her to Tokyo, where she'd closed a deal that had seemed impossible. The rich gray and orange was for personal travel—weekends away, spontaneous getaways that reminded her that life was more than just work. It had accompanied her on a spontaneous trip to the Maldives, where she'd finally allowed herself to relax after months of non-stop work. These bags weren't just luggage; they were symbols of the life she'd built for herself, a life that was, in many ways, the opposite of the one she'd known growing up.

Yet despite her meticulous planning and the security these items provided, there were moments when the weight of them became almost unbearable. *She would stare at her collection, feeling a tension between pride and burden, a dichotomy that was becoming harder to reconcile.*

Even in her travel essentials, RoKo's need for abundance was evident. It wasn't about materialism; it was about preparedness, about the comfort of knowing she would never be caught off guard.

Her mother often lamented, asking, *"Are there no other colors left for you to buy?"* But RoKo knew it wasn't about the colors—it was about the reassurance that came from having options, from knowing that she had enough.

This need for abundance wasn't born out of greed or vanity; it was rooted in something much deeper. Growing up, limited resources and the strong mindset of saving for rainy days were the norm. The lack of choice, the constant need to make do with less, had left a mark on her young mind. *It was these memories that fueled her desire to fill her life with choices, with an abundance that would ensure she never had to feel the sting of scarcity again.*

As she grew older and began to carve out her own path, RoKo found success in ways she had never imagined possible. But with that success came an unexpected undercurrent of fear—*a fear that the abundance she had worked so hard to achieve might slip through her fingers one day just as easily as it had eluded her family in the past. This fear, though rarely acknowledged, began to influence her choices.*

RoKo realized that her habit of buying in multiples wasn't just about having more; it was about creating a buffer against the unpredictability of life. In a world that often felt chaotic and uncontrollable, having choices, having multiples, was her way of exerting control over at least one small corner of her existence.

It was as if by owning more, she could somehow shield herself from the uncertainty that life inevitably brought. Each pair of shoes, each business suit, each carefully chosen item in her collection was a talisman against the unknown—*a way of saying to herself,* "I am prepared. I have enough. I am in control." *But the psychology of it went even deeper than that.*

RoKo began to see that her need for multiplicity was also tied to her sense of self-worth. *Growing up with so little had left her with a persistent sense of inadequacy, a feeling that no matter how much she achieved, it would never be enough to fill the void left by those early years of scarcity.*

But the more she bought, the more she began to question: Was this abundance truly fulfilling her, or was it simply masking deeper insecurities?

Her colleagues admired her impeccable taste and the effortless way she carried herself. To them, she was a symbol of success and sophistication, a woman who had it all figured out.

But beneath the surface, her habit of buying in multiples was more than just a preference—it was a reflection of her journey from scarcity to abundance, a mindset of abundance.

To others, her lifestyle might have seemed excessive, but to RoKo, it was simply an expression of who she was—someone who knew what it was to have little and had made the conscious decision to live a life of plenty. Her lifestyle often drew attention—enough and more.

This chapter of multiplicities was just one thread in RoKo's intricate life—*a life woven with both strengths and imperfections,* continuously evolving as she discovered herself through the things she cherished and the world she meticulously crafted around them.

But somewhere in the back of her mind, RoKo knew that the true adventure lay not in the things she collected but in discovering what she could let go of. The real challenge, she realized, would be in learning that her worth wasn't tied to what she owned but to who she was.

The final, most difficult step would be confronting these truths head-on, perhaps with the help of others, like a therapist, though RoKo was far from ready to take that step.

RoKo measured her success and self-worth through luxury and status, using high-end brands as markers of her achievements, *with each new purchase serving as a reminder of how far she had come.*

Her deep attachment to these possessions brought her a sense of stability, but it also kept her caught in a cycle—where the joy of each new purchase faded quickly, leaving her hungry for the next.

It was like chasing a fleeting high, always needing more to fill the void. In the end, her relationship with material things wasn't just about owning nice things; it was part of a much bigger, more complicated journey—one where she was trying to express who she was while searching for something that truly made her feel fulfilled.

RoKo knew that if she ever went to a therapist, the notes might read something like this: *"Patient exhibits a strong compulsion towards collecting luxury items..."* She could almost picture the therapist's pen scratching across the paper, diagnosing her attachment to material things as a symptom of something deeper, more unresolved. The thought of it made her smirk—*wasn't everyone just trying to fill a void?* But as much as she brushed off the idea with humor, a part of her knew there was truth in it.

So if RoKo indeed would have gone, this is what the notes probably would have looked like:

Patient Name: **Roshni Koshy**
Occupation: **Executive**

Presenting Concerns:

- *RoKo exhibits a strong compulsion towards collecting luxury items and high-end accessories, viewing them as essential extensions of her identity and tools for self-expression.*

- *She meticulously curates her belongings, indicating perfectionistic traits and a need for control over her environment.*
- *Despite her material abundance, there is evidence of dissatisfaction, leading to a continuous cycle of seeking new items—a classic case of the hedonic treadmill.*
- *RoKo's self-worth appears heavily tied to external validation, raising concerns about potential identity diffusion.*

Psychological Observations:

- *Obsessive-Compulsive Traits: RoKo's behavior shows patterns of obsessive-compulsive tendencies, particularly in her need for order, control, and perfection. These traits may contribute to her stress and create barriers in her interpersonal relationships.*
- *Materialism and Identity Issues: The patient's reliance on material possessions as markers of self-worth suggests underlying struggles with identity formation. These items might be her way of compensating for a lack of internal stability and self-assurance.*
- *Hedonic Adaptation: RoKo's constant pursuit of new acquisitions indicates a cycle where initial pleasure from new items quickly fades, driving her to continuously seek more.*
- *Underlying Anxiety: Her compulsive behaviors and perfectionism could be rooted in deep-seated anxiety and fear of inadequacy, possibly stemming from past experiences of scarcity or low self-worth.*

Therapist's Advice to RoKo:

1. *Understanding the Root Causes:*

   - *Therapy Recommendation: Engaging in cognitive-behavioral therapy (CBT) could help explore the emotions driving your compulsive behaviors and attachment to material objects. This process may uncover the deeper need for control and perfection.*

- ○ *Mindfulness Practices: Starting mindfulness techniques might help you become more aware of your thoughts and behaviors, recognizing when you're using material possessions to cope with underlying emotional issues.*

2. *Reframing Self-Worth:*

   - ○ *Internal Validation: Shift focus from external validation to building a sense of self-worth from within. Identify core values and strengths that are independent of material possessions or others' perceptions.*
   - ○ *Self-Compassion: Practice self-compassion by acknowledging your worth beyond what you own or achieve. Daily affirmations, journaling, or reflecting on non-material accomplishments can foster a healthier self-view.*

3. *Challenging Perfectionism:*

   - ○ *Embrace Imperfection: Challenge your need for perfection by intentionally allowing small imperfections in your life. Perhaps not curating every aspect so meticulously or accepting that not every possession needs a specific purpose.*
   - ○ *Set Realistic Goals: Establish more balanced goals that allow for personal growth and flexibility, rather than rigid perfection.*

4. *Reducing Material Attachment:*

   - ○ *Declutter and Simplify: Consider decluttering by letting go of items that no longer serve a meaningful purpose. This can reduce the emotional weight attached to possessions and create space for more fulfilling experiences.*
   - ○ *Focus on Experiences: Shift energy and resources toward experiences rather than possessions. Investing in relationships, hobbies, and personal growth can offer more lasting satisfaction.*

5. *Building Emotional Resilience:*

    ◦ *Emotional Awareness: Pay attention to your feelings when drawn to new acquisitions. Ask yourself if this is fulfilling an emotional need that could be addressed more healthily.*
    ◦ *Support Networks: Strengthen support networks by building deeper, more meaningful relationships. These connections can provide emotional support and reduce reliance on material possessions for comfort.*

6. *Future Follow-Up:*

    ◦ *Regular Check-ins: Regular follow-up appointments are recommended to monitor progress and adjust the treatment plan as needed. Together, we can work toward a more balanced, fulfilling life that isn't reliant on material excess.*

In another reality, maybe those notes would sit in a neat little file, tucked away somewhere in a therapist's office, like one of the many curated items in RoKo's life. But for now, they were just a hypothetical—an amusing thought experiment she entertained briefly before moving on, continuing her journey in her way, for better or worse.

TWO

THE ENIGMA OF ARMAAN (AV)

Armaan wasn't a man easily understood. On the surface, he seemed like the kind of person who had life all figured out—confident, successful, and unflappable. His presence commanded attention in any room he walked into, not because he sought it, but because it seemed to follow him naturally. Whether it was the way he carried himself, with a subtle but undeniable air of authority, or the way his eyes seemed to assess everything around him with sharp, analytical precision, AV was someone who left an impression.

But beneath this composed exterior was a man of contradictions, a tangle of emotions that few ever got to see. AV was a master of compartmentalization, an expert at keeping the different parts of his life in neat, separate boxes. His professional life was one of those boxes—perfectly organized, meticulously planned, and fiercely protected. In the corporate world, AV was known for his strategic mind, his ability to see the big picture without losing sight of the details. He was the kind of leader who inspired both respect and fear, someone who could make tough decisions with a calmness that belied the weight of the choices he made.

But as sharp as his mind was, there was a part of AV that was deeply guarded, even from himself. This was the part of him that longed for connection, for something real and lasting, but was too afraid to reach for it. He had built walls around his heart—walls so high and so thick that even he sometimes forgot what they were protecting. It wasn't that he didn't want love or that he didn't care—on the contrary, AV cared deeply, more than he would ever admit. But the vulnerability that came with love was something he couldn't bear, something that made him feel exposed in a way that nothing else did.

AV's relationships were often marked by this tension between desire and fear. He would let someone in, just enough for them to feel close, but not enough to see the full extent of his inner world. His charm, his wit, his intelligence—they were all part of the mask he wore, a way to keep others at a safe distance while still appearing open and engaged. *To those who didn't look too closely, AV seemed like the perfect partner—attentive, thoughtful, and always in control. But for those who tried to dig deeper, who sought to understand the man behind the mask, there was a sense of frustration, a feeling that no matter how close they got, there was always a part of him that remained out of reach.*

This was the paradox of AV—he was both deeply present and yet, somehow, always a little bit absent. He had a way of making you feel like the most important person in the world when you were with him, but the moment you were apart, you couldn't shake the feeling that he had already moved on, that his mind was somewhere else entirely. It wasn't intentional, this emotional distance; it was simply the way he had learned to protect himself from the pain of disappointment, of loss, of getting too close only to be let down.

In moments of introspection, AV would sometimes wonder why he was like this. He knew, on some level, that his fear of vulnerability was holding him back, keeping him from experiencing the kind of the love, excitement, and thrill he secretly longed for in life.

But the thought of opening himself up, of letting someone see all the parts of him—the strengths and the pieces still in progress, the confidence and the quiet doubts—was terrifying. Yet, he kept his distance, even when it hurt, even when deep down, he knew it wasn't what he truly wanted.

There were times, late at night, when AV would lie awake, thinking about the choices he had made, the people he had let slip away. *He would replay conversations in his mind, wondering if he had said the right thing, if he had pushed too hard or not hard enough. But by morning, those thoughts were neatly packed away, filed under "things to deal with later."* AV was too practical, too focused on the future to dwell on what might have been. Regret, he told himself, was a luxury he couldn't afford.

But for all his careful planning and attention to detail, AV couldn't shake the constant feeling of restlessness. It was like something important was always just out of reach, slipping away before he could grasp it. This unsettled feeling drove him to work harder, to succeed, to be the best at everything he did. But each success felt empty, every win seemed to fade quickly, leaving him unsatisfied, like no achievement was ever enough. Maybe he was just too serious, always trying to control everything. He needed to relax, let go a bit, and embrace the unpredictability of life.

In relationships, this restlessness manifested as a need for control, a desire to dictate the terms of engagement. He wanted to be close, but only on his terms. He wanted to be loved, but without the messiness that love so often brought. *This need for control often led to misunderstandings, to moments where his partners felt shut out, confused by his seemingly contradictory behavior.* But for AV, it was simply the way he navigated the complexities of his own emotions—a balancing act between intimacy and independence, connection and protecting one's own peace.

At his core, AV was a man who yearned for something more, even if he wasn't always sure what that "more" was. He was a man who loved deeply but struggled to express it, who cared profoundly but was afraid to show it. He was a man of great intellect and ambition, but also carried profound doubts and anxieties. *And though he often appeared to have it all together, there was a part of him that was always searching, always questioning, always wondering if he would ever find the peace and fulfillment he so desperately sought.*

And so, AV moved through life, a complex, enigmatic figure—both strong and vulnerable, confident yet uncertain—always striving for more. To the world, he was a man of success, dynamism and stature, but to those who looked closer, he was more than he appeared—a man of complexity, with hidden depths and a quiet yearning that he couldn't easily express.

It was this very depth that made AV so intriguing and frustrating, yet also so deeply human—a man who, like all of us, was trying to find his way in a world that often felt too big, too chaotic, too unpredictable. But unlike many, AV carried his search with quiet dignity, a strength drawn not from having all the answers, but from his relentless pursuit of them.

Just like RoKo, AV had a particular affection for his shoes. He was an Adidas fan through and through, collecting pairs like others might collect rare art. To him, they were more than just footwear—they were companions on his journey. Each pair told a story, every scuff and crease a testament to the places he'd been, the meetings he'd walked into, and the streets he had wandered. From limited-edition collaborations to classic designs, AV curated his collection with a discerning eye. His favorites were always the understated models, like the sleek black Stan Smiths he wore for important meetings or the bright, retro-inspired Superstars he slipped on during weekends. For AV, Adidas wasn't just a brand; it was a lifestyle—one that symbolized simplicity, style, and durability, values he held close in his personal life as well.

His friends often joked that the shoes were his "silent partners," always there to ground him, both literally and figuratively. While some people showed off their collections of expensive watches or cars, AV's collection of Adidas shoes reflected his personality: grounded, practical, yet with a subtle touch of flair.

His blue linen jacket was almost a second skin, worn so often that his EA used to joke she could pick him out in a crowd just by the sight of it. She had seen him in maybe three or four other colors, but the blue one was his signature, a color that seemed to match his calm demeanor.

He looked ravishing when he wore his royal dark blue suit with his brown leather shoes, like something out of a fashion magazine, drawing admiration wherever he went.

But to top it all was his military print bomber jacket that truly captivated his best friend, Tia. There was something about that jacket—maybe it was the way it hugged his broad shoulders, or the way the print seemed to echo the strength and resilience she admired in him. She often teased him about stealing it away one day, saying it was the perfect mix of rugged and stylish, just like him.

"You know," she would say with a playful glint in her eye, "One day, that jacket is going to disappear, and you'll have to come find it. But good luck getting it back." He would laugh, knowing full well she meant it, and secretly enjoying the idea of her wearing something that was so distinctly his.

AV might have had a modest wardrobe compared to RoKo's abundance, but what he wore reflected who he was—classic, dependable, and with a touch of flair that made him stand out without even trying. The clothes, the shoes—they weren't just items; they were a part of his identity, much like RoKo's collections were to her.

And just Like RoKo, if ever, though he never would, but if at all ever, or just for the sake of argument AV did visit a therapist, this is what the therapy notes at the clinic will look like.

Patient Name: **Armaan Vaidya**
Occupation: **Entrepreneur**

Presenting Concerns:

- *AV exhibits strong tendencies towards control and emotional detachment, often keeping others at a distance.He views independence as essential to his identity, resulting in difficulty forming deep, emotional connections.*
- *He meticulously plans and organizes his life, indicating a perfectionistic drive and an inherent need to maintain control over every aspect of his environment, whether it's his work, his relationships, or his personal space.*
- *Despite his outward confidence, there is evidence of internal conflict and dissatisfaction, particularly in his personal relationships, where his fear of vulnerability leads to a cycle of withdrawal and isolation.*
- *AV's self-worth is heavily tied to his achievements and the image he presents to the world, raising concerns about potential identity issues and emotional detachment from his true self.*

Psychological Observations:

- *Perfectionistic Drive: AV demonstrates a strong desire for perfection, particularly in his professional life. This need for control may stem from a fear of failure or rejection, driving him to maintain a facade of success and emotional strength.*

- *Emotional Detachment and Control:* The patient's difficulty in forming deep connections suggests an underlying fear of vulnerability. AV's reliance on control and emotional distance could be mechanisms to protect himself from perceived emotional risks.
- *Identity and Self-Worth Issues:* AV's strong attachment to his achievements and outward persona indicates a struggle with self-acceptance. His need to project an image of success may be compensating for an underlying lack of self-assurance and internal validation.
- *Avoidance and Withdrawal:* AV's tendency to avoid emotional conversations and withdrawal from relationships when they become too intense suggests a fear of intimacy. This avoidance pattern could lead to further isolation and dissatisfaction in his personal life.

Therapist's Advice to AV:

1. *Understanding Emotional Detachment:*

   - *Explore Emotional Barriers:* Engage in therapy to explore the emotional barriers that lead to detachment in relationships. Understanding the root cause of your avoidance in expressing emotions and forming deep connections will be essential in building healthier relationships.
   - *Cognitive-Behavioral Therapy (CBT):* Consider CBT to identify and challenge the thoughts that contribute to emotional detachment. This therapy could help in altering patterns of behavior that push people away, including those stemming from past experiences or fears of vulnerability.

2. *Building Emotional Intelligence:*

   - *Emotional Awareness Practices:* Work on becoming more aware of your own emotions and the emotions of others. Practices like journaling or mindfulness can help you connect with your *feelings and better understand how they influence your behavior.*

- *Active Listening: Practice active listening in conversations, especially with loved ones. This can help in building empathy and understanding, allowing you to connect more deeply with those around you.*

3. *Reframing Relationships:*

- *Value Emotional Connections: Shift your perspective on relationships to see them as opportunities for growth rather than potential threats to your independence. Understand that emotional intimacy doesn't diminish your strength but can actually enhance it.*
- *Set Boundaries with Compassion: Learn to set and communicate boundaries in a way that is firm yet compassionate. This will help in maintaining your autonomy while also respecting the emotional needs of others.*

4. *Challenging Perfectionism and Control:*

- *Embrace Vulnerability: Recognize that vulnerability is not a weakness but a necessary part of meaningful relationships. Allow yourself to be open to the uncertainties of relationships, understanding that this is where true connection happen*
- *Accept Imperfection: Work on accepting that neither you nor your relationships need to be perfect. Let go of the need to control outcomes, and instead focus on being present and authentic in your interactions.*

5. *Reducing Avoidant Tendencies:*

- *Address Fear of Intimacy: Explore any underlying fears related to intimacy and commitment. Therapy can provide a safe space to discuss these fears and develop strategies to manage them without resorting to avoidance.*

- *Gradual Exposure: Start with small steps in opening up emotionally. Gradually allow yourself to be more vulnerable in your relationships, beginning with close friends or a therapist, before extending this openness to romantic partners.*

6. *Enhancing Self-Compassion:*

- *Practice Self-kindness: Engage in self-compassion practices that focus on treating yourself with the same kindness you would offer to others. This can help in reducing self-criticism and building a more positive relationship with yourself.*
- *Reflect on Achievements: Regularly reflect on your strengths and achievements, not just in your career but also in your personal growth. This can help reinforce a sense of self-worth that isn't solely tied to external accomplishments.*

7. *Future Follow-Up:*

- *Regular Check-ins: Schedule regular follow-up sessions to track your progress and adjust the treatment plan as needed. Therapy is a journey, and ongoing support can help you navigate the complexities of emotional growth and relationship dynamics.*

Therapist's Closing Note:

Embrace the Journey: AV, the journey toward emotional growth and healthier relationships is not an easy one, but it's one that can lead to a more fulfilling and balanced life. Remember that it's okay to take things one step at a time. The important thing is to keep moving forward, to keep challenging yourself to grow, and to remember that you are capable of forming deep, meaningful connections without losing yourself in the process. You have the strength to change, and with the right tools and support, you can build the life and relationships you truly desire.

THREE

AND THE STORY BEGINS! THEIR FIRST NIGHT TOGETHER...

From the moment they met, it was as if RoKo and AV were kindred spirits, colliding in a universe that had been waiting for their encounter. Earlier that evening, they had both been at a celebration at Alloro, the beautiful Italian restaurant in a posh Bengaluru hotel—separately at first, each at their respective tables, cheering for friends and strangers alike. Though they had unknowingly crossed paths before, it wasn't until the after-party that their true connection began.

The celebration RoKo was attending was entirely separate from the one AV was part of—they were there for different reasons, unaware of each other's existence until that moment, simply sharing the same physical space, unaware—completely unaware.

RoKo had hosted a client dinner at Alloro, and afterward, she joined a group of close friends celebrating a birthday in another part of the restaurant, happy to relax in their familiar company. Meanwhile, AV was across the room, attending a corporate dinner to toast his company's successful year.

As the evening's main event wound down, and the lively chatter began to fade, the host at one of the tables, with a twinkle in his eye, casually extended an open invitation to an after-party. The offer was tossed out to nearly everyone at the restaurant, like confetti, catching a few curious glances and raised eyebrows. But as with any spontaneous gathering, no one knew for sure who would actually show up. The host, still expecting only a modest turnout, figured it would just be a small, intimate group by the end of the night.

But something about the night, or perhaps the spontaneity of the invitation, drew RoKo in, even though she hadn't planned to accept. It was as if an unseen force was nudging her into the unknown, pulling her toward something—or someone—she couldn't yet foresee.

RoKo was a vivacious whirlwind, a bundle of contagious energy that could light up any room. At the party, she had moved effortlessly through the crowd, connecting with everyone—both, those she knew as friends and those she was now getting to know as friends of friends. Her laughter was infectious, and her curiosity boundless. With her presence, the atmosphere instantly brightened, and those around her couldn't help but be drawn to her captivating charm. Despite the crowd, she was fully present, engaging in conversations that made everyone feel important. She had a knack for making people feel at ease, with an insatiable zest for life.

Behind her lively exterior, she carried deep empathy and a passion for understanding the world and the people in it. She had this uncanny ability to spark engaging conversations that left people feeling both understood and inspired.

In essence, RoKo was a force of nature—a dynamic blend of energy, empathy, and intellect. Her presence was a gift to those fortunate enough to know her, and her influence left a lasting impression on everyone she met. She had a way of staying in people's minds—somehow, she always had a high recall value. Amidst the many interactions at the party, she was intrigued by the variety of people and stories, but one person, in particular, kept catching her eye.

AV, on the other hand, was her perfect foil—a tall, handsome introvert with an air of quiet confidence and a mind sharp as a razor. He, too, had been at Alloro for most of the evening, though his presence was more reserved. He preferred observing to speaking, often standing on the periphery of social gatherings, absorbing the nuances that others missed and finding solace in the patterns and logic that others often overlooked. At the party, he remained on the edges, quietly taking in the scene, but RoKo's vibrant energy kept drawing his attention.

In essence, AV was a perfect mix of intellect, introspection, and understated passion. As he observed RoKo at Alloro, he felt a pull—a connection he couldn't quite explain, but one that felt strangely familiar. It was as if his quiet confidence, grounded nature, and sharp mind naturally gravitated toward her vibrant energy, creating a dynamic interplay of opposites that seemed almost orchestrated by fate.

RoKo, too, felt something stirring inside her. She decided to go to the after-party, though she couldn't quite explain why—not even to herself. Perhaps it was curiosity, or maybe the residual energy of the evening. She didn't dwell on it; she simply felt drawn to continue the night. With a quick glance around the room and a subtle shrug, she found herself heading toward the after-party, unaware of what lay ahead.

And their first real interaction happened almost by chance. As RoKo breezed into the room designated for the after-party, her eyes sparkled with curiosity and mischief. "Looks like there's some serious P&L discussion going on," she remarked, her voice cutting through the air with surprising depth. Abhinav and Armaan—known among friends as "The A & The A"—paused, drinks in hand, and turned to her in astonishment. They exchanged a look, marveling at how a stranger could read the undercurrents of their conversation with such precision.

Neither knew who she was, and she knew nothing about them. Yet, in that moment, it felt as if an invisible force had connected them all. It was like a sudden clap of thunder—an electrifying presence that you feel in your bones before you fully comprehend what it is. They stood there, seeing it, feeling it, experiencing it, and yet struggling to understand the magnitude of what had just happened.

AV, almost fixated and grounded in his chair, couldn't help but be drawn into the moment. Until then, he had been on the fringes of the party, he and Abhinav still deeply engrossed in the laptop screen. But RoKo's insight and energy pulled him in, making him feel part of something larger. The room was charged with a shared energy that none of them could explain, but they all sensed it: something extraordinary had begun. It felt as if the higher realms had been planning this moment for a long time, and now, finally, it was happening.

People often say that things happen when they are destined to, but that doesn't absolve us from putting in the effort. AV could sense this undeniable truth—there was a magnetic pull in the air, an unseen force drawing them all together in ways they couldn't fully comprehend.

Destiny had led them to this moment. They had sensed something drawing them together long before their paths actually crossed, though they couldn't quite understand what it was. Now, standing almost side by side—they could feel it: the magic, the magnetism, or perhaps the significance of it all. It was a blend of fate and choices, creating a powerful and inexplicable attraction, one they were only just beginning to notice, pulling them closer without them fully knowing why.

But how had they not noticed each other earlier? Had they made it happen consciously? Both would have denied it vehemently if asked. Perhaps they hadn't even seen each other consciously until this very moment. Or had they? AV recalled fleeting glimpses of RoKo throughout the evening—moments when their paths almost crossed but didn't. They had unknowingly crossed paths several times, oblivious to each other's presence, and yet here they were, caught in a surreal wave of unknown excitement.

In that moment at the after-party, it felt as if a mystical energy had enveloped them—a deep, profound connection that transcended mere chance. RoKo's mind grappled with the unknown, trying to piece together what might unfold. She had never felt anything like this before.

Up until this point, RoKo had not noticed AV's strong and unmistakable presence in the room as much. Or rather, she hadn't paid attention to the quiet figure on the sidelines. Lost in her own world of joy, she had caught sight of him, but he was just another face in the crowd, a fleeting glance among many.

But now, something had shifted. With AV catching almost her entire attention, everything felt different. Her energy filled the room, vibrant and magnetic, drawing everyone—including AV—into a shared space of warmth. The room buzzed with her charm, an intangible force that seemed to captivate everyone, as if they were under a spell, and suddenly, AV was no longer just a face in the crowd.

RoKo had decided to attend the gathering on a whim, unsure if she truly wanted to go but drawn in by the lively energy of the after-party in Bangalore. She hesitated at first, feeling a slight disconnect as most of her friends opted for street food and pub-hopping adventures. The vibrant Bangalore night pulsed around them, yet something about this particular group pulled her in—a camaraderie that seemed inviting in its own unique way. As the only older woman among a crowd of younger men eager to unwind, RoKo was acutely aware of the age gap, but rather than feeling out of place, she embraced it with the same grace she carried in every aspect of her life.

From the moment she entered the room, the dynamic shifted slightly. Her presence commanded a quiet respect—her effervescent personality blended effortlessly with the relaxed atmosphere, making her feel both welcomed and significant. The men around her, caught up in their laughter and casual banter, seemed intrigued by the way she fit so seamlessly into their circle. She noticed their fleeting glances of curiosity, but she didn't mind. RoKo had always believed that connection transcended age, and tonight she intended to prove it.

As the evening progressed, the conversation took a deeper turn. What began as light-hearted jokes and surface-level banter evolved into meaningful discussions about life, career, and the intricacies of modern relationships. RoKo found herself sharing stories—glimpses of her journey through corporate boardrooms, balancing ambition with vulnerability, and finding joy in the little things. The group listened, captivated by her insights, drawn to her wisdom without feeling lectured. Her laughter blended with theirs, filling the room with warmth.

Time slipped away unnoticed, and before long, the late hour crept into her consciousness. A fleeting sense of reality settled in—she was in a room full of men, most of whom she had just met, and it was getting late. Yet, there was no discomfort, no sense of unease. Instead, she felt a strange contentment, as if she had added something intangible to the night, leaving her mark on the conversation and the energy of the group.

As the night wore on, RoKo knew it was time to say her goodbyes. With a graceful farewell, she rose from her seat, her movements deliberate but unhurried. She wished them well on their various adventures—some heading off to explore more of the night just like the rest of her friends, others settling into quieter discussions. Her smile lingered in the air, the final touch of her enchanting presence, as though she had left a piece of herself behind in that room, a quiet echo of the warmth she carried with her.

As RoKo stepped out of the room, the cool air from the hallway brushed against her face, she paused for a moment, feeling the weight of the evening—a subtle, satisfying sense of connection that transcended age or circumstance. She hadn't planned on making an impression, but as she walked away, she knew she had. The night, like so many before it, had offered her something unexpected—a reminder that sometimes, the most profound connections arise from moments where we least expect them.

Inside, the energy of the evening lingered, resonating in the room. The men stood there, feeling the afterglow of an extraordinary encounter, each one silently acknowledging that they had witnessed something remarkable. RoKo's departure left them impressed—whether by her acumen, her wit, or the unique energy she brought to the evening—creating a memory that would not soon fade.

And yet, as RoKo made her way back to her room, a nagging curiosity about the quiet man she had barely spoken to—AV—tugged at her thoughts. She couldn't help but wonder why she felt so inexplicably drawn to him, despite their brief encounter.

As she reached for the door and swiped her key card, the lock blinked red. "Oh, come on!" she groaned, throwing her head back in disbelief. Not again. She muttered the words under her breath, louder this time. She had just gotten the card fixed—what was this, a running joke? The red light blinked back at her as if mocking her, daring her to try again. With a sigh, she leaned against the doorframe, the silence of the hallway making her frustration all the more ridiculous.

The day's exhaustion weighed heavily on her, and the thought of trudging back to reception felt daunting. Each step felt like twenty as she dragged herself down the hallway. When she finally reached the front desk, she mustered a tired smile and politely asked Tutu to reactivate her card. Tutu, the ever-cheerful front desk manager, greeted her with the same calm and friendly demeanor, even at this late hour. Efficient as always, Tutu reactivated the card in no time, handing it back with a reassuring smile.

Now, almost in a state of deep slumber, her eyes weary and her mind foggy, RoKo stumbled back towards her room. She couldn't help but still think of AV—how strange it was that she felt drawn to him. She could barely stay upright, her body yearning for the warm embrace of her comfortable bed, ready to sink into sleep. As she reached her floor and approached the door, a flicker of recognition jolted her awake, fully awake as though she had seen a ghost. To her right stood AV, his room impossibly close, right next to hers. For a moment, she questioned reality, pinching herself and wondering if she was hallucinating, wondering if her mind had brought him to life like a vision.

Really, right next door in this vast, large—yeah, large—huge, rather humongous big—no, ultra-big, bigger-than-big sprawling hotel? she thought incredulously.

Was this merely a coincidence again, or yet another twist of fate?

She had noticed him fair and square at the after party, but the idea of him being so close now seemed too strange to be random.

Was there no other room available? Could it be really possible that there were no other rooms available than the one right next to hers, or a room for RoKo away from his? The notion sent a warm tingle down her spine, as though fate was weaving their paths together again and again and again.

Their eyes met, and a silent understanding passed between them. They exchanged smiles and a quiet goodnight. RoKo felt a flutter of excitement in her stomach, like a thousand butterflies taking flight. Her inner voice chimed in, and out of those thousand butterflies, 999 whispered, "Hey RoKo, you're falling in love again —once again, yeah, just one more time. It feels so damn right. This is your love again at first sight."

She quickly snapped out of the mental chatter, her heart racing as she tried to grasp where she was—was this just a coincidence, or something far deeper? RoKo's hands trembled as she fumbled with her key card, her thoughts swirling. The card slipped from her fingers, clattering to the floor. She cursed under her breath, snatching it up quickly. With a shaky breath, she swiped it again, praying the door would unlock this time. The door lock, which had stubbornly blinked red earlier, suddenly turned green, leaving her no reason to linger in the hallway any longer. Just as she was about to step into her room, the silence was broken by a voice—AV's.

Hey he said out aloud, I'm headed out. Let me know if you need anything.

She paused, her heart hammering. A part of her longed to ask for his time to unravel the mystery of their connection, the mystery of that pull she felt, but instead, she replied with a polite, Thanks for asking. Have a good one. I shall retire now; I've had quite a day.

AV paused, standing still for a moment right there at the doorway, eyes searching her's for any hint of what might come next.

He silently willed her to speak, his chest constricting with the overwhelming need to hear her voice—just one word, anything to break the silence, anything to keep her from slipping away.

He wanted her to invite him inside, to offer him a coffee or, even better, a cold beer to prolong the night until dusk hit dawn. But the words never came. The moment stretched, then quietly slipped away, leaving his unspoken hopes hovering in the air, unfulfilled and fading as she stepped back into her room.

And on the other side of it all, inside her room, RoKo moved like a shadow, her body heavy with exhaustion as she slowly peeled off her clothes. She tossed them aside carelessly, letting each piece fall to the floor like remnants of the day. She drifted toward the bathroom, the cool air brushing against her bare skin as she paused in front of the mirror. Her reflection stared back at her, distant, her mind replaying the brief but electric encounter with AV. What is it about him? she wondered, unable to shake the thought.

Seeking an escape from her own swirling thoughts, she stepped into the shower, the hot water spilling over her like a wave. The steam rose around her, fogging the glass and enveloping her in a cloud of warmth. For a moment, the tension in her body eased, but even the pounding of the water couldn't wash away the image of AV from her mind. His face lingered, refusing to be drowned out by the steady stream cascading over her.

Reluctantly, she stepped out of the shower, wrapping herself in a towel as the cool air hit her skin once more. She moved slowly, as if weighed down by the thoughts swirling in her mind, slipping into her pajamas with the hope that sleep would finally take her. But it remained just out of reach, teasing her. She lay in bed, her heart still racing, her mind still chasing images of AV, the man who seemed to have unknowingly taken hold of her thoughts.

Despite her best efforts, her thoughts kept drifting back to Armaan, like leaves caught in a gentle breeze. His presence lingered, like a shadow at sunset, and the memory of their brief encounter at the after-party replayed in her mind, like a song she couldn't get out of her head. There was something about him, something that tugged at the edges of her soul, a pull she couldn't quite name. She wanted to resist, to push it aside, but like a moth drawn to a flickering flame, she found herself helplessly circling back to him, unable to let go of that enduring tie. Little did she know, playing with fire would seal her fate, just as it does for the moth.

As she lay in bed, staring at the ceiling with her tangled thoughts, she couldn't shake the memory of his innocent smile or the way his eyes seemed to hold entire worlds within them. The feeling that their paths were connected in some way and the sense that their lives were meant to merge stayed like the aftertaste of fine wine, rich and heady, intoxicating her thoughts with every sip of memory.

Was this more than just a momentary attraction? The cosmos felt close, whispering secrets she couldn't quite grasp. What was it trying to tell her? What did it have in store for them next? The questions wove through her mind like a restless tide, pulling her deeper into the unknown, refusing to let her find peace.

As her thoughts spiraled like smoke from a flickering candle, she whispered to herself, *"If it's meant to be, and I really don't know why but, he'll knock on the door tonight. Somehow, I just know he will."* With that whispered declaration, she finally surrendered to sleep, her mind still haunted by images of AV. Hours slipped by in eerie stillness, until suddenly, a sharp knock on the door shattered the silence, startling her awake with a jolt, her heart racing as if the universe had answered her call.

It was late, the hour well past midnight, and the unexpected sound sent a shiver through her. She heard it again, more insistent this time, echoing in the stillness of the night. The unusual knock, rather than the ring of the doorbell, added to her disorientation.

Rubbing her eyes, she tried to call out, Hang on, coming, though her voice emerged weak and groggy from the depths of her slumber. The darkness in the room pressed down on her, making the hallway light spilling through the peephole appear even brighter.

Trusting in the hotel's security, she stumbled to the door, her movements guided only by the faint glow of the hallway light, not bothering to switch on the lights. With a mixture of trepidation and curiosity, she turned the handle and pulled it open.

Her breath caught in her throat as she found Armaan standing right there, his expression a whirlwind of concern mixed with something else—something she couldn't quite name.

Seriously, again? she thought, feeling a rush of adrenaline as she took in the sight of him. Am I dreaming? What is he doing here? What is this? What are we up to? What do I want? What does he want? The questions tumbled in her mind. Why does he keep coming back? And why has he suddenly transformed from the distant Pluto to the blazing Mercury in my cosmos, revolving around me, completing five orbits in less than five hours?

And in all actuality and literally as if reflecting her inner turmoil, the hallway light cast long shadows, deepening the intensity of the moment. Their eyes met, and the charged air between them buzzed with unspoken words and the heavy weight of possibilities. The silence was so intense, so palpable, neither dared to break it.

AV took a tentative step forward, his gaze unwavering. 'Were you sleeping?' he asked softly. 'I got you a drink. I noticed you having one earlier, and when I realized the hotel didn't have a minibar and the restaurant was closed, I picked one up on my way back. I thought you might want one as well, and just in case if you did, you wouldn't be able to get it here, he explained, his voice low and earnest.

RoKo was taken aback, completely caught off guard. This gesture—unexpected and different—was more than she ever imagined.

Though part of her wanted to tease, Oh, yeah, yeah, who sleeps at 1 a.m.? I was just waiting for you to knock on my door since I had called upon the universe, hoping you would. Deep down, however, she could feel it—this was exactly what she had wished for before drifting off to sleep, a silent wish that had somehow brought him to her door.

But keeping those thoughts to herself with a smile, RoKo said, "Oh, that's so strangely unexpected of you," rubbing her eyes and absentmindedly smoothing her hair.

Before her mind could catch up, her heart took control, and the words spilled out: "Now that you're here, why don't you come in?" The words hung in the air, heavier than she'd intended, carrying an invitation to more than just a room. She was bewildered by her own actions tonight; first, she had ventured into an after-party filled with random strangers, engaging in conversations amid a room full of half-drunk men, and now, here she was, at nearly 1 a.m., inviting a stranger into her room.

Wow, this is exactly what I'd been waiting for, AV thought, his nerves tingling. He'd wanted her to invite him in—needed her to—almost as much as she had.

He stood there, a bottle of red wine in one hand, another drink in the other, and a backpack slung over his shoulder. She realized she knew nothing about him—not who he really was, where he came from, or anything beyond the surface. It felt reckless, yet oddly fitting. RoKo was bold, but this was a new level of crazy. This was Another Level Shit. Roko level ALS, as she called it.

To her surprise, AV didn't hesitate. It was as if he had been waiting for this very moment, longing for it in a way that seemed almost predestined. Without a word, he stepped inside, his movements sure and swift, as if he feared the invitation might be rescinded if he delayed even a second longer.

He settled on the sofa while she took a seat in the chair opposite him. Their eyes locked once more, this time with an intensity that seemed to strip away all distractions, leaving only the raw energy between them. The silence was thick, almost tangible, charged with the weight of unspoken words and hovering curiosity. The surreal nature of the moment—the sheer strangeness of it all—began to creep in, but neither was willing to shatter the connection. Sensing the charge between them growing stronger, RoKo decided to take control, breaking the spell with a soft smile. 'Hey, thanks for my drink. What's in your glass?'

He smiled, a hint of something unsaid visible in his eyes, and replied, Oh, I call it RuCo—Rum with Coke, but tonight, it's just Coke. With everyone out there at that lively after-party, it's hard to be the one without a glass in hand. He paused, his gaze locking onto hers with a quiet intensity. I hope you don't mind that—or me knocking on your door at this hour, he added, his voice dipping into a tone that seemed to carry more meaning than the words themselves.

RoKo wanted to say, Oh, not at all! Trust me, I was just waiting for you to knock. I had declared to the stars, the universe, the cosmos and to myself before sleeping that you would show up tonight. But just as the words were about to spill out, one sane butterfly out of the thousand fluttering inside her kicked some sense into her, halting her confession. Instead, she simply smiled, keeping the truth to herself and letting the unspoken linger between them, and then......She burst into a fit of laughter that echoed through the room. Still giggling, she looked at AV and asked, "Wait, what did you say? Can you say it again?"

To her, it almost sounded like her name—as if he had said RoKo. And again, the 999 butterflies inside her stomach shouted at the top of their voices, See, he even knows your name! We told you it's love again, the nth time but yeah, love at first sight, so so bright, feels so right, just like a thousand stars shimmering in the twilight. Amidst all this chaos, the one wise butterfly tried to stay calm, wanting to catch a wink, but ended up saying, 'Here goes RoKo.'

In the meantime, amidst RoKo's mental chatter, with a mischievous glint in his eye, Armaan repeated, I call it RuCo.

Armaan was perplexed by what he had said that had sparked this burst of delightful laughter. He hadn't seen anyone laugh so freely, so openly, in what felt like ages. And now, he couldn't tear his gaze away from her, captivated by the way she laughed with such abandon.

Was it the name of the drink that amused her so, or was there something more? He wasn't sure, but the sight of her laughing filled the room with a warmth that made him question if it was simply a funny name or something deeper.

As her laughter finally began to subside, RoKo clutched her stomach, feeling the ache from laughing so hard. The laughter faded into a thoughtful smile, a strange mix of amusement and curiosity flickering in her eyes. The similarity between the names—RuCo and RoKo—felt like more than just a coincidence.

It was uncanny, as if fate had a hand, well meaning and well intended hand in crafting this moment. The thought stayed on, adding a touch of mystery to the evening.

They hadn't even exchanged names until now. Armaan had no idea that the woman sitting across from him, in her sleepy yet graceful state, was named RoKo. With a hint of mischief in her eyes, she decided to end the suspense. Hi, I'm Roshni Koshy, but my friends call me RoKo, she said, and as the words left her lips, both of them burst out laughing again, the bond between them deepening with every shared laugh.

The room seemed to join in their laughter, its walls subtly vibrating with the shared mirth, as if it, too, recognized that this was no ordinary encounter. There was an undercurrent of something deeper, something both of them sensed but couldn't quite grasp. It felt as though the very air around them was charged with an unseen force, guiding them together. The coincidence was too uncanny, too perfectly aligned, as if fate itself had carefully crafted this moment, leaving them both captivated with the mysterious forces at play.

Breaking the silence, Armaan felt the need to introduce himself, to step out of the shadows of being just a random stranger—though, after their paths had crossed so many times that evening, he didn't feel like a stranger anymore. 'Hey, I'm Armaan Vaidya. Some of my friends call me AV, others just V.'

As he spoke, their eyes locked once more, and for a flash of a moment, it felt as if the universe itself had conspired to bring them together repeatedly, and would continue to do so, until they truly noticed each other and found themselves in each other's presence, weaving their destinies into a single thread.

They did not know each other, yet an unspoken sense of ease enveloped them as if they were old souls reconnecting across the ages. It was as though they had known each other for much longer than these few brief hours. It was as though their paths had crossed in past lives, finding each other once more. The air between them was charged with an irresistible energy that transcended time and space, hinting at a destiny far greater than they could fathom.

The room seemed to grow quieter, the world outside fading away as they looked at each other. The dim light cast soft shadows, accentuating the surreal quality of the moment. RoKo felt a slight shiver run down her spine, not from cold, but from the overwhelming sense of affinity that pulsed between them. AV's fingers brushed against the edge of the table, and he felt a faint tingling in his fingertips, as if the energy of the moment had somehow transferred into his very being.

Every glance, every shared breath, seemed to deepen the unspoken bond between them, drawing them closer to a truth neither was ready to fully acknowledge. It was as if the room itself had become a witness to their interaction, holding its breath in anticipation of what might happen next. Their hearts beat in unison, a steady rhythm that echoed the unspoken promise of something far greater than either of them could yet understand.

Could it be that this stranger was meant to be more than just a passing acquaintance? It was as if their souls recognized each other, entangled in a story written by the universe itself. In that fleeting moment, everything seemed possible—a strong bond formed, as if their very essences had been waiting for this union all along.

It was as if the universe itself had been working toward this moment, bringing them together in a way neither could have anticipated. This chemistry felt ancient, as if their souls had been searching for each other through countless lifetimes. It was hard to tell if this meeting was a coincidence or the inevitable reunion of two spirits who were always meant to find each other, across time and beyond.

And then they realized someone had to break the silence.

Hey RoKo, AV began, his voice laced with curiosity, a sly grin playing on his lips. Tell me, how did you know that Abhi and I were deep in discussion about a P&L? Was it a wild guess, your intuition, or are you secretly a psychic? He leaned in closer, his tone dropping to a whisper, Because let me tell you, after you left, you were still the topic of conversation. You left everyone in awe, and I'm pretty sure no one's going to forget you anytime soon. Maybe not ever. His eyes twinkled with a mixture of admiration and intrigue as he spoke, clearly enjoying the game.

RoKo couldn't help but laugh, filling the room with a warmth that made the moment feel even more special. She raised an eyebrow, feigning innocence, but the glint in her eyes betrayed her enjoyment of the compliment.

AV leaned back, a little more relaxed now, as if sharing a secret. And let me tell you, he continued, I'm glad you showed up when you did because we were in the middle of trying to salvage a real BROKEN P&L. It was a mess, and none of us had a clue how to fix it or change the trajectory. Your timing was impeccable—a much-needed distraction, and quite the charismatic and audacious one at that.

RoKo flashed a knowing smile, a silent acknowledgment of the power she wielded in that room, even if only for a moment.

She looked up at AV, her eyes sparkling with amusement. Well, I wouldn't say I'm psychic, she teased, but I do have a knack for knowing when to make an entrance.

AV chuckled, appreciating her wit. You certainly do, he agreed, lifting his glass in a celebratory toast, To timely entrances and the mysteries they bring.

AV, then with a subtle nod, hinted for RoKo to get a glass for herself and start pouring the drinks. RoKo hesitated, a flicker of caution crossing her mind—she didn't want to wake up to a reality she hadn't chosen, next to a stranger she barely knew.

But AV's presence was more intoxicating than anything she could pour into a glass. Perhaps it was the alluring scent of his cologne, or the way his smile curved just so, revealing that irresistible dimple on his cheek. Maybe it was the way he carried himself—confident yet mysterious—that clouded her judgment. It was as if his entire being was a potion she couldn't resist.

Almost as if under a spell, RoKo rose and fetched two fresh glasses one each. She returned, the clink of the glass like a quiet agreement between them. Here's to two strangers, she thought in her mind, though the word 'stranger' hardly seemed to fit anymore. In that moment, AV wasn't just anyone—he was something more, something she couldn't quite name.

And with a teasing grin, she raised her empty glass and said, Here's to two strangers— who V can't RoKo!

The words seemed to hang in the air for a split second before they both burst into laughter yet again, a laughter so infectious and uncontrollable that it echoed through the walls. Their names, so perfectly connected in that moment, became the catalyst for a fit of giggles that spiralled into something much more.

The laughter grew louder, more uninhibited, until it reached a point of no return. It filled the room, spilling out into the hallway, so much so that the occupant next door, in a mix of annoyance and curiosity, had to call the concierge to send someone up and quiet them down. But in that moment, RoKo and AV were lost to the world, caught up in the joy of their unexpected link, where even their names were enough to bind them in this shared, unbreakable moment.

AV was as dazzled by RoKo's presence as she was intoxicated by his. There was a strong magnetic draw between them, a deep yearning within him to know her more, to explore the connection that was sparking between them. He was almost four drinks down, though his composed demeanor revealed nothing of it and RoKo also knew nothing of it—he remained the perfect gentleman, fully aware of where he stood in the moment.

AV, being the gentleman he was, poured them each a drink, and they finished their first one rather quickly, eager to pour another, letting a few more inhibitions slip away. With a casual glance at the thermostat, AV remarked, Hey, is it just me, or are you feeling cold too, RoKo? Feeling cold, even though the room was set at a comfortable 24 degrees, RoKo smiled and replied, Looks like it's just you.

He chuckled softly, his voice lowering as he teased, Hmmmm, must be the wine. Mind if I get under the sheets? This chill is creeping in on me. The suggestion hung in the air, subtle yet laced with an undercurrent of something more, leaving RoKo to wonder just how far this night might go.

Huh!! RoKo's mind raced with confusion. Seriously? In my room at this hour, sharing an unplanned drink, and now he wants to get into my bed? She thought, Why doesn't he just go back to his room? She couldn't help but wonder what was really on his mind. Is he even aware of what he's saying, or is it just the wine talking? She pondered!

She almost offered to change the temperature or turn down the AC for him, but instead, the words that slipped out were, Okay, if you think that would make you feel comfortable.

And to this, the one wise butterfly fluttering in her stomach whispered, Seriously, RoKo? You want a stranger in your bed? This is the height of desperation. What are you up to? This isn't right—you need to have some foresight.

Without a moment of hesitation, AV moved to the bed, settling comfortably under the warm duvet that still carried the subtle scent of RoKo from earlier that evening. He felt an odd sense of comfort and familiarity, a strange déjà vu struck him, as if he had lived this moment before—uncertain when, but knowing he had. Snapping himself out of it and re-engaging in the conversation, he casually asked, So, RoKo, what do you do for a living?

But before she could respond, he added, Hey, isn't it just too quiet in here? Mind if I put on some music?

RoKo's mind was spinning now, faster than the Earth orbiting the Sun, faster than the Moon circling the Earth, faster than the planets dancing through the cosmos. This is getting crazier by the minute, she thought. First, the unplanned drink in the middle of the night, then he's under my sheets, and now he wants music? The situation had escalated far beyond anything she had expected, bordering on surreal.

She couldn't help but wonder, What's next? The only thing left seemed to be for him, to pull her close, feel her breath warm on his skin, and let that undeniable charm of his take over.

But that wasn't all, RoKo also was far from her usual self, finding herself saying yes to every request that came from AV. This wasn't who she normally was—she was always strong-willed, with a clear sense of boundaries, she was literally intimidating in her persona for most men. Yet tonight, she couldn't seem to resist him, as if a spell had been cast over her, growing stronger with every passing moment, making her agree to things she would ordinarily question.

Little did she realize that this uncharacteristic behavior would be the very thing to create turmoil between them, should they spend days, weeks, or even months together. It was as if, in her effort to keep the peace and hold onto the connection she felt with him, she was already sowing the seeds of future discord.

RoKo loved music herself, but Armaan, without waiting for an affirmative, was already on YouTube, playing an English song she didn't recognize. It didn't bother her much; after all, this wasn't some romantic date where the music and the lyrics needed to be perfect. At this moment, the songs were there just to fill the silence, rather the very brief momentary awkward pauses if at all between their conversations.

However, after every song, an ad would play—some mischievous, perhaps due to the late hour or influenced by AV's browsing history. That's when RoKo suggested switching to Apple Music, which AV didn't use, and he quickly shot, 'Okay, why don't you play some music on your phone?

Being a true music lover, RoKo carefully selected a playlist of beautiful melodies and soulful Hindi songs, each one carrying a story of its own. The music filled the room, soft and soothing, as though it were wrapping them in its gentle embrace. The familiar tunes seemed to resonate with both of them, evoking memories and emotions they hadn't even realized were there.

As the songs played, they found themselves humming along, their voices naturally blending with the tunes. It felt effortless, as if they had shared this moment many times before, the music drawing them closer, speaking in a language deeper than words.

The third glass of wine was poured, and AV casually asked for another bottle of water. The atmosphere in the room shifted, growing warmer and more intimate, the music quietly building a bridge between them, one that words couldn't.

As they shared stories, they realized how deeply the music connected them. Both of them had sung these songs during their college days—sometimes to their crushes, other times when they missed someone, or even when their hearts were broken.

For both AV and RoKo, these songs had served as band-aids for their emotional wounds. The more they talked, the more they discovered how much they had in common, far more than either had imagined.

For RoKo, AV seemed like a male version of herself, embodying everything she had hoped to achieve in life. He had already done the things she dreamed of—serving in the forces, seeing the world, keeping his body fit and strong with a discipline she admired. He carried himself with a confidence that was both natural and inviting. He had learned new languages, experienced different cultures, and made lifelong friendships along the way. The way he spoke about his journey, with passion and humility, stirred something deep within her—a sense that he had lived the life she had always craved, but never quite reached. There was so much more to him that she wasn't yet aware of but would get to know in the coming months.

As they spoke more, they began to see each other as reflections of one another, like two halves of a soul split into different bodies to create a perfect balance. It was as if they were meant to find each other, to bring together the pieces of themselves that had been missing. It felt as if the stars had aligned just right, guiding them to this moment, to complete a story that had been written long before they met.

And suddenly, RoKo's attention shifted to the song playing in the background. Her laughter faded, and a pensive expression took over. The sparkle in her eyes dimmed as if she had just remembered something painful.

Noticing the change, Armaan gently drew her closer—not in their physical reality, but through the tenderness in his eyes and the quiet calm of his voice—as he softly asked, 'Hey, what happened? Where did you go just now?

Pulling herself out of that thought, RoKo forced a smile and replied, 'Oh, nothing important. So, what were you saying?'

But AV wasn't letting it go that easily. 'No way,' he insisted, leaning in with genuine concern. 'I could see it on your face—where did you go just now? Tell me. Bolo, bolo. Say everything that was running through your mind, all that you were just processing in that brilliant brain of yours.

RoKo hesitated, her smile softening. She took a long, deep breath, the weight of her memories filling the air. 'This was the song my first boyfriend and I used to listen to and sing together a lot,' she finally admitted, her voice rich with nostalgia and warmth.

Ahaan! First boyfriend, you say? So, there's probably a long list hidden somewhere, isn't there? AV's voice carried a cheekyl lilt, his eyes twinkling with a mix of excitement and curiosity. I can just picture it—a list of all the lucky ones you indulged in, and maybe even a few poor souls who could only dream of getting close. I bet there were some who spent hours working up the nerve, only to lose their courage the moment they saw you. He chuckled softly, the teasing in his tone making the moment light and easy.

By now, RoKo was three drinks in, and she was already captivated by the way AV had said Ahaan. Most of her inhibitions had melted away, her usual guards lowered. Here was someone she felt an irrefutable pull toward, and he was praising her—how could she not revel in that?

Seriously? she teased back.

Oh yes, AV replied with a grin. Look at yourself. You dress like someone in charge—crisp white shirt, navy blue coat, the whole deal. No man would have the guts to just walk up to you and strike up a conversation without knowing you first. You're intimidating, you know that, right?

RoKo raised an eyebrow, half-amused and half-confused. Little did she know, AV had noticed her earlier in Alloro when she was fully immersed in her business mode, dressed to impress while closing a big deal and hosting a client dinner with no time to change for the birthday party and deciding to be there in her usual avatar. She had assumed he would praise her for that, for her professionalism, but now she couldn't quite tell if he was complimenting her or being sarcastic.

If I'm that intimidating, then what made you knock on my door? she asked, a touch of agitation creeping into her voice as she tried to decipher his intent.

AV chuckled softly, shaking his head. Intimidating? Nah, not to me—or okay, let me admit, maybe just a little, he teased, leaning in slightly, his confident grin never wavering. You've got that spark, that mystery—I couldn't stop myself from coming closer. It was as if my legs were moving on their own, and I just had to see where they'd take me. But that gloomy face, let me tell you, has no place here tonight! I need to hear it all—the whole story, every single detail. And don't forget the highlights!

RoKo couldn't help but laugh at his persistence, though her heart pounded louder with every second. Seriously, AV, you're just too much, she retorted, her voice dripping with mock exasperation. Yet beneath the surface, a whirlwind of 999 flirtatious butterflies fluttered wildly, screaming inside her, Just tell him you love him! Say it, RoKo, say it! Her outward resistance was deliberate, but every moment of his attention felt electric, like sparks flying in the air between them, and she was secretly savoring every second of it.

AV leaned in closer, his expression both teasing and earnest. Come on, I'm all ears. Don't leave me hanging now. How else am I supposed to know if I have to measure up to some legendary first boyfriend?

RoKo rolled her eyes but felt a warmth spreading through her, a mix of amusement and the unspoken chemistry between them. Alright, alright, she sighed dramatically, but only because you asked so nicely.

She couldn't deny that his genuine interest and light-hearted humor were making it impossible to keep her guard up. As she began recounting the story, she felt the nervousness from earlier melt away, replaced by the easy, lighthearted banter that seemed to flow naturally between them.

You know, RoKo began with a wistful smile, there are moments when I still think about the happy times we had together, and, of course, the bittersweet ones too. But honestly, I'm so relieved it didn't work out. She paused for effect, her eyes sparkling with a mix of humor and gratitude.

Why is that? AV asked, clearly amused by the statement.

Oh my god, AV, you have no idea—living with him and living up to his expectations would have been just impossible, he needed a caretaker more than a life partner! And to top it all off, she leaned in as if sharing a secret, he's now got this big, fat tummy and a thinning hairline. Can you imagine?!

She exhaled with exaggerated relief, as if releasing the last remnants of that past relationship, I'm so glad we broke up, she added with a mock shudder, her expression one of calm relief. Dodged a bullet there!

AV chuckled, shaking his head. That's so mean of you to say, but it sounds like you got out just in time! I mean, you're practically glowing with relief. I just hope you haven't shared this with him and broken his heart again, because losing you wouldn't have been easy on him.

RoKo laughed, carefree enjoying the way AV's teasing made her feel at ease, and the 999 butterflies inside her laughed too, whispering excitedly, See, see, see, he likes you too.

Exactly! RoKo continued, I've never been happier to have my freedom. Who knew the creator was doing me a favor back then? She paused, a sly grin tugging at her lips. And yeah, I told him—not directly, but you know how it goes—we both knew we're poles apart. And not just a little different, like North Pole and South Pole different! She burst out laughing, her energy lighting up the moment.

We still meet up now and then, grab a drink, and catch up—nothing too dramatic. It's strictly the friendly shoulder kind of deal. You know, the let's laugh about how we dodged that bullet kind of friendship. No romantic escapades, no sparks flying—just a quick toast to how much better off we both are. She winked, the grin widening. We clink our glasses, share a few stories, and call it a night. Honestly, it's nice knowing we're better as distant poles. It's all fun and games when you're sitting at opposite ends of the Earth. The North pole and the South pole like they are meant to be, always and always yeah meant to be.

AV leaned back, still grinning. Well, here's to fate, then—his fate, in all its sadness. And to you—glad you made it through with your spark still intact!

Yeah, those college days filled with that innocent, head-over-heels kind of love, RoKo began, her tone light and carefree as she reminisced. The kind of love where everything felt larger than life. You know, the kind where just a glance from across the room could send your heart into overdrive, and holding hands felt like the universe was aligning just for you. Sharing an ice cream? That was a monumental moment, like we were conquering the world together, one scoop at a time.

I must admit, he was a total sweetheart—still is, actually. There's something comforting in knowing that even though we didn't make it as a couple, I still gained a friend for life.

She leaned in slightly, her eyes sparkling with mischief. I mean, who would've thought, right? We went from holding hands in the cafeteria, hearts racing over the smallest gestures, to holding onto a friendship that's stood the test of time. It's funny how life works like that.

I know that if I ever need anything, he's just a call away. I didn't keep him as a boyfriend, but I definitely hit the jackpot with a lifelong friend. And honestly, how many people can say that?

RoKo's smile widened as she kept going, full of praise, He's just so genuine! With him, I can be completely myself—vulnerable, bare soul and all. There's no pretending, no holding back. He just gets me. There's no judgment, just this unspoken understanding that I can be as weird or wild as I want, and he'll still be there, steady as ever.

She leaned back, her eyes sparkling with warmth. It's like having a safety net, she mused, knowing you've got someone in your corner who understands you on a level that goes beyond words. RoKo's voice softened. I might have lost a boyfriend, but I gained something even better—a friend who makes me feel totally at peace, like I can finally breathe easy around someone. And let's be honest, that's way better than some half-baked romance any day!

She paused, took a deep breath, and continued with a laugh, my friends used to tease me endlessly for his name was Lokesh, and they'd joke, RoKo, go RoLo! Oh my god, it became such a thing! We commuted on the same college bus, and the moment he'd board, they'd start with, Hey, why so sad, sad ho toh RoLo?

RoKo's laughter bubbled up again, as if the memories were playing out in front of her. And that wasn't all. They made it their mission to come up with ridiculous scenarios, like RoLo running off into the sunset together or naming our imaginary kids after planets—Jupiter and Venus. Every single day, it was something new, some absurd little story they cooked up to keep the joke alive.

By the end of the semester, it felt like I was starring in a sitcom just like the Rahul and Anjali of Kuch Kuch Hota Hain, just that here it was RoKo and LoTa in their RoKo ka LoTa, and RoLo was the punchline. Even the bus driver got in on it at one point! It was like a running gag that never got old.

And wait, wait, it's not over yet! The funniest part of the whole story is still to come—his full name was Lokesh Tayadey, but everyone called him LoTa. Looking back now, it was the perfect nickname for him, especially with that perfectly round pot belly of his. She burst out laughing, the memory lighting up her face, and AV couldn't help but join in, his laughter blending with hers.

And at times, RoKo continued, wiping tears of laughter from her eyes, his friends would shout, Hey, LoTa, don't RoKo me, I gotta go! Turning into a joke that, no matter how ridiculous, always had us laughing crazy.

AV shook his head, grinning. Sounds like you had quite the characters around you, he said, still chuckling at the story.

Oh, absolutely, RoKo agreed, her smile wide and warm. Those were the days, filled with fun and endless inside jokes that just never seemed to get old. Every day felt like a new episode of comedy, and no matter how silly it got, we laughed like it was the first time we'd ever heard it. Even the smallest thing could send us into fits of laughter. It was the kind of carefree joy that only comes with being young, with nothing to worry about except how much fun you can have in the moment.

The last time we met, he got all sentimental, opening up about how he wished things had turned out differently. He told me how he still thought about what could have been if we hadn't broken up, how he wondered what our lives would look like now if we'd stayed together. It was like he was stuck in this little 'what if' bubble, replaying those memories in his head.

He kept going on and on about how much he missed what we had, and the whole time, I was sitting there, nodding politely, but in my head, I was doing a little victory dance, thinking, Thank goodness we didn't end up together! I mean, I get it—it was all about that cute, first-crush kind of love and all that—but I couldn't help but feel a wave of relief that I had dodged that bullet, she finished with a playful wink leaning back in her chair.

Alright, enough about me! she said. I'm sure you can see the relief written all over my face now. So, let's turn the tables—tell me about yourself. How were your college days, Mr. Armaan?

Did you have your own version of puppy love, or were you too busy charming everyone with that smile of yours? Her eyes sparkled with curiosity as she eagerly awaited his story.

And in that brief moment of silence, the wise butterfly became pensive, thinking, Okay, this is the second time now—second strike for both, and yes, I'm counting. Who else would do the job, anyway? The other 999 are already lost in a haze. Now, back to the point—are RoKo and Armaan already flirting with each other? Are these subtle compliments actually hints? Or is there something else going on in their minds?

AV's remark echoed in the butterfly's thoughts, I bet there were some who spent hours working up the nerve, only to lose their courage the moment they saw you. Later, he added, I just hope you haven't shared this with him and broken his heart again, because losing you wouldn't have been easy on him.

And now, RoKo was dancing to the same tune, joining this unexpected mutual admiration society, asking with a teasing smirk, Were you too busy charming everyone with that smile of yours?

Is it flirting? Or is it just being friendly? Or is it simply a case of two people mutually appreciating each other? The wise butterfly pondered, sensing that something more was unfolding subconsciously, even if neither AV nor RoKo fully realized it yet.

AV laughed at RoKo's statement and replied, Hey, haven't you realized yet? I'm not exactly someone who gets noticed as much as you do. You have this ferocious spitfire energy around you that practically shouts, Come talk to me! You'll get energized just by being in my presence—and trust me, I'm not here to intimidate anyone! He laughed out loud, the sound filling the room.

AV, stop being a spoil sport, RoKo shot back with a gleam in her eye. If that's your answer, maybe it's time to pull the sheets over and drift off into slumber.

Oh, you're welcome, darling, AV teased, I'm already under the sheets, and I wouldn't mind you joining in.

RoKo shot him a look of disbelief mixed with silent rage.

Okay, okay, don't intimidate me! AV giggled again, trying to defuse the atmosphere with humor.

So, where do you want me to start? Should we take a little stroll down your memory lane, just one more time? AV teased, a naughty sparkle in his eye.

Huh? What do you mean? RoKo replied, a hint of irritation creeping into her voice.

Well, AV began with a smirk, you mentioned Lokesh had bulked up into a heavy lifter. I was in that zone too—just shed 7 kilos off this body, and here I am, aiming to drop 5 more.

Oh, really? RoKo's irritation melted into curiosity as she raised an eyebrow.

Yep, AV continued, but unlike Lokesh, I'm keeping it lean and mean. Didn't want to lose my edge, you know? Gotta stay sharp for charming all those lovely ladies. He winked, his tone light and teasing.

Is that so? RoKo shot back, her mood lifting as she played along.

Well, I guess you're doing a great job then, aren't you?

I try, AV replied, his smile widening as the lighthearted exchange flowed effortlessly between them, witty remarks diffusing the tension and adding a touch of mystery to their evolving chemistry.

RoKo looked at him in surprise, thinking to herself, Seriously? Six foot two, with a well-built, gym-sculpted body—defined abs and perfectly chiseled biceps, all hidden beneath his shirt but impossible not to notice. Where did you even lose 7 kgs from? And where would you find another 5 to lose?

She couldn't hold back the disbelief in her voice. Are you serious? she blurted out, her eyes scanning him with skepticism. I don't believe you at all.

Oh, you need to, RoKo, AV replied, his tone suddenly taking on a more serious edge, a subtle intensity that hadn't been there before.

High time you start believing me... and believing in me.

Huh? What did you just say? RoKo's brows furrowed in confusion, her demeanor faltering for a moment.

AV blinked, as if he himself was unsure where those words had come from, almost as if a higher voice had spoken through him. He hadn't intended to say anything like that, yet there it was, hanging in the air between them, thick with unspoken meaning and mystery.

RoKo's mind raced, trying to grasp the sudden shift in tone. Was there something deeper here, something more than just playful banter? The atmosphere in the room seemed to change, charged with an undercurrent

Ahaan! heyyy, nothing, AV quickly backtracked, I said, believe me, I lost 7 kgs. But RoKo wasn't convinced, her eyes narrowing in suspicion.

Hmmm, maybe I haven't seen you in the right light, RoKo teased, her voice full of mischief. Mind stepping out of my bed? I'd like to take a proper look at you... up close, from head to toe!

Huh? What did you say, RoKo? AV responded, his eyes widening in surprise at her unexpected suggestion. There was a light, spirited energy between them, something they hadn't quite felt in a while. The challenge was inescapable, leaving them both curious about what might happen next.

RoKo extended her hand toward AV, a lazy grin on her face. Come on, show me where you shed those 7 kgs, she teased, her tone matching the easy banter they had going on.

AV chuckled as he got up from the bed, standing tall with a knowing smile. Alright, alright, he said, turning around as if preparing for a grand show. RoKo, you're really making me dance to your tunes tonight.

RoKo leaned back, crossing her arms with a mock-serious look. Hmm, well, why don't you give me a little spin? Let me see if I'm convinced.

A spin? AV sighed, dramatically throwing his hands up, though the smile on his face gave him away. Really? You want me to do that?

Yeah. She wants you and yeah she needs you, can't you sense it, you moron AV, muttered the 999 butterflies.

Oh, absolutely, I need you RoKo replied with a mischievous twinkle in her eye.

You need me?? remarked AV.

Seriously AV, that's what you hearing. I need to see if you're telling the truth! I need you to do the ramp walk. You're practically a model! RoKo exclaimed gleefully, her eyes sparkling with delight.

Without missing a beat, AV obliged, giving her not just one, but three spins of a perfect cat walk in the room. RoKo couldn't help but admire him, her smile growing wider with each turn.

She savored the moment, enjoying every second of watching him until he finally stopped and said, Okay, Madam, is that enough, or do you want more of me?

A little bit more said RoKo.

AV laughed, shaking his head. You're impossible, you know that?

RoKo shrugged, her smile growing wider. And yet, here you are.

Their wordplay was heating up, each exchange more charged than the last.

That'll be all, AV, RoKo announced after 4 rounds of his dazzling catwalk, raising her hand for a high five. AV eagerly met it, their hands connecting with a satisfying slap.

And when their hands met for that high five, something unexpected happened—a jolt of energy surged through them, sparking something magical. It wasn't just a casual touch; it was electric, sending goosebumps up their arms.

They both felt it, a mutual recognition that this was more than just playful banter. For a brief moment, they locked eyes again, each silently acknowledging the intensity of what had just passed between them.

Realizing they were teetering on the edge of something that could spiral out of control, they instinctively pulled back, trying to ground themselves before the moment swept them away.

I admire your effort, said RoKo with a smile. And since we're out of drinks, how about a Coke? she asked, still smiling.

But Armaan the charmer, ever the one with a plan, had a secret up his sleeve—or rather, hidden in his bag. He had smuggled not just a bottle of red wine into the room, but also a bottle of Rosé.

You know, he said with a sly smile, I thought one might not be enough, so I came prepared. The mischievous spark in his eye indicated that he had a feeling this night might require a bit more than just conversation.

RoKo raised an eyebrow, a mix of amusement and curiosity washing over her yet again. Oh, so you came more than fully equipped, didn't you? she teased, feeling the atmosphere between them shift to something lighter, though no less charged.

AV nodded, reaching into his bag to reveal the bottle of Rosé. I thought we could use a change of pace, he said, as he began to uncork it. The soft pop of the cork was like a release, signaling the start of something both were eager to explore.

The night was still unfolding, and they were working their way through the second bottle of wine.

As AV uncorked the bottle, he couldn't help but add with a smirk, Also, if I have your permission, may I slide back into your sheets, ahhhh I meant the sheets, Your Highness? His tone was teasing, and RoKo couldn't help but smile at his boldness.

But, as usual, AV didn't wait for an answer—he was already back under the covers, getting comfortable in her bed before she could even respond.

The atmosphere felt alive with anticipation as the wine filled their glasses, the pink liquid almost signaling the start of something different. The scent of the wine mixed with his lingering perfume, creating a blend that filled the room and wrapped them in a mysterious, exciting atmosphere.

Little did she know, the scent of his perfume would stick with her long after he was gone, a reminder of a night that was just starting to unfold. It would linger on her pillow, in her thoughts, and in the air around her, making her think back to this unexpected spark that felt both thrilling and just a bit dangerous.

As they settled back, the silence between them wasn't awkward anymore but full of possibilities. The sheets rustled as AV made himself comfortable, his presence filling the space with a warmth that felt both familiar and new. RoKo couldn't help but wonder what exactly had she welcomed into her life tonight.

They had just started to explore this strange, compelling energy between them, but it was clear that whatever came next was going to be something neither of them had planned for. The wine was just the beginning, a hint of a night that would stay with them long after the last glass was finished.

Well, you're quite the distractor, AV, RoKo remarked, You say you don't attract attention, but let me tell you—I'm sure you do, and not just a little, but plenty.

She leaned in slightly, her tone teasing yet curious. We were just getting into talking about you, getting to know you, and here you go again, steering the conversation away from yourself.

AV couldn't help but chuckle, recognizing her persistence. The back-and-forth between them was like a game, each move carefully considered yet effortlessly executed, leaving both wondering where this verbal sparring would lead next.

So yeah, tell me more, RoKo urged, leaning in with a curious smile.

I told you the truth, and you should start believing me, at least now, for I aint that much of a stranger any longer considering I am in your bed the second time, AV replied with a playful wink yet again.

I was one of those not-so-talkative, definitely not attention-drawing kind of boys, AV began, a hint of nostalgia in his voice.

I was tall—rather, I am tall, as I'm sure you've noticed. I was taller than most boys my age, and the girls barely reached my shoulder. And let me tell you, tall and lean isn't exactly what you'd call candy to the eye.

RoKo couldn't resist interjecting, Oh, I agree with that!

AV looked at her in disbelief, a mock-serious expression on his face. Ahaan, seriously? he exclaimed, the familiar phrase rolling off his tongue with ease.

By now, RoKo had fallen in love with his signature Ahaan and couldn't help but mirror it with her own Seriously!

Anyway, AV continued, a smirk playing on his lips, I hardly spoke to girls. But I remember this one Valentine's Day, I had a girl come over to my house and drop off a letter and flowers.

Trust me, I had the time of my life trying to convince my parents that I had nothing to do with it. I did not even know the girl's name until I saw it signed at the bottom of the letter.

RoKo burst out laughing, imagining the awkwardness of the situation. Oh, I can only imagine the look on your face!

AV chuckled along, shaking his head at the memory. Yeah, it was something. My parents were convinced I was hiding some secret romance. But really, I had no idea who she was. Just goes to show, even the quiet, unnoticed boys have their moments, I guess.

Oh, apart from that, I've had quite a time with my gang of boys, AV continued, a reminiscent smile playing on his lips. We were a tight-knit group, and let me tell you, we had some of the best times together.

None of us had girlfriends, so there was no pressure of Valentine's Day or Friendship Day or any of those days where you're supposed to be all romantic and stuff.

He paused, his eyes twinkling as he recalled one particular story. There was this one time during Holi. You know how it is, right? Total chaos, everyone's out on the streets, armed with colors, water balloons, and pichkaris. Well, my gang decided to take it up a notch. We made this giant water balloon slingshot out of old bicycle inner tubes—one of the guys had seen it in a movie and thought it would be hilarious to try it out.

RoKo leaned in, intrigued. And? How did that go?

Oh, it was a total hit—literally! The AV show really shook things up, AV laughed, the memory still clear as day. We set up on the roof of our building and started launching these massive water balloons at the kids playing in the street below. The first few splashes were epic—kids running in every direction, trying to dodge what they thought were ordinary water balloons. But when they looked up and saw us with our DIY slingshot, they were both impressed and furious!

He continued, his laughter infectious. Of course, it didn't take long for the neighborhood uncles to notice, and soon, we had a mob of angry aunties chasing us down the stairs, yelling that we were going to flood the whole colony. We scattered in every direction, trying to escape the wrath of the aunties and uncles.

It was pure chaos, but also so much fun. We ended up hiding in a friend's garage, covered in colors and out of breath from laughing so hard.

RoKo chuckled, shaking her head. Sounds like you guys were quite the troublemakers.

Oh, we were, AV agreed, his smile broadening. But those were the best days, no worries, no responsibilities—just us boys, creating memories and having the time of our lives.

And yes, AV added with a sheepish grin, the day didn't exactly end on a high note. We got quite the thrashing when we got back home.

RoKo laughed, picturing the scene. I can only imagine! But it sounds like it was totally worth it.

Absolutely, AV nodded, the nostalgia evident in his voice.

Worth every single scolding.

And where are all of them now, that gang of yours? RoKo asked, her curiosity piqued.

Oh, we all make it a point to meet at least twice a year, AV replied with a fond smile. One meet is usually here in the country, where we revisit our old haunts and laugh about the crazy things we used to do. The other meet is our way of exploring new places together—we pick a destination, pack our bags, and just go. It's our way of keeping the spirit of those carefree days alive.

Even though life has taken us in different directions, whenever we get together, it's like nothing has changed. We relive those golden memories, and in the process, we create new ones that are just as wild and fun.

RoKo could see the warmth in AV's eyes as he spoke about his friends, and it made her smile. That sounds amazing, she said, imagining the kind of bond they shared. It's like you guys have this unbreakable relationship, no matter how much time has passed.

Yeah, it's pretty special, AV agreed, his voice softening. We've been through a lot together, and those friendships are a big part of who I am today.

RoKo leaned in, her curiosity getting the best of her. Aren't you one of a kind, AV? Having fun, enjoying life, and making the most of it, she remarked with an innocent grin. But tell me, any regrets? Anything you wish you could change if you could go back in time?

AV paused, his usual light-hearted demeanor shifting as he considered her question. You know, life's been good, and I've tried to live it with no regrets, he began, a thoughtful expression crossing his face. But if I had the chance to go back, maybe there are a few things I'd do differently. Sometimes I wonder if I could've been more open, more vulnerable with the people who mattered. Maybe there's a conversation or two I wish I'd had, decisions I'd rethink.

RoKo listened intently, not realizing how much this moment would come to mean to her in the future. One day, she would find herself yearning for AV to ask her the very same question—so she could shout, Yes, yes, yes! There's one thing, just one thing I would change if I could. But for now, in this passing moment, she was oblivious to the twists and turns that awaited her, unaware of the depth of her own future regrets.

And the last statement shifted something within AV, for a moment, it seemed as though a flash of the past flickered in his eyes. He grew slightly uncomfortable, his usually relaxed demeanour tightening just a bit. RoKo noticed the change but decided to act as if she hadn't.

Instead, she casually said, Hey, pass me the bottle of water, please, hoping to lighten the energy and steer him away from whatever thoughts had unsettled him.

AV, still lost in his thoughts, absentmindedly reached for the bottle and was about to hand it to RoKo when he realized it was empty. Oh, I'm sorry, I didn't realize it's empty, he said, looking at the bottle. They had run out of water, leaving them with nothing but the wine.

Let me call the concierge, AV offered, quickly picking up the phone and dialing zero. RoKo felt a sense of relief as the sound of the dial tone seemed to pull him out of his reverie. But when no one answered, AV dialed again, this time with a hint of irritation creeping into his demeanor. I'll just grab some bottles from my room, he said, standing up with surprising agility despite the four glasses of wine he'd already consumed making his count of drinks almost eight.

As he made his way to the door, he called out over his shoulder, Don't close the door—I don't want to have to knock again. I'll leave the double lock on, so you don't have to get up. And by now, I'm sure you know I care for you.

The words stayed in the air long after he had left, echoing through the room with an unexpected weight. I care for you? Seriously? RoKo thought, her mind racing. I hardly know you, and you hardly know me. We've just shared a few stories and some laughs, and now you care for me?

The 999 butterflies who were quiet just until now inside her stirred once more, now wide awake and buzzing with a mix of confusion and excitement. He cares for you, they whispered. And you... you love him already. Keep up the good work, RoKo.

The room, now silent except for the echo of his words, seemed to hold its breath, as if waiting to see what would happen next. RoKo's heart was working overtime, and she couldn't deny the flutter of feelings that had taken root, feelings she wasn't sure she was ready to confront.

AV was quick to return, breezing back into the room with two bottles of water, a pack of mixed nuts, and something that caught RoKo's eye—a sleek pack of Wrigley's Rain gum.

The gum had a certain flair to it, almost like a status symbol, and it struck RoKo that it probably cost more than most would think.

With a suspenseful grin, AV handed her one of the bottles and the gum, saying, These are my favorite, but hey, let's get something in our stomachs first before you start chewing away. I command it! He added with mock seriousness, causing both of them to break into laughter.

RoKo, catching on to the joyful mood, decided to keep the game going. "As you command, my CO," she teased, using the military acronym for Commanding Officer. The light-hearted banter remained in the air, filled with warmth and vibrant energy, as both of them clearly were enjoying the teasing exchange.

They settled back down, munching on the nuts, but something more than just humor was a part of the room now. The shared joke, the easy laughter, and the familiarity that had slipped into their conversation all hinted at a deeper connection, one that was still unfolding, layer by layer. RoKo couldn't help but wonder how it was possible to feel so at ease, yet so intrigued by someone she had only just met. The mystery of it all was intoxicating, making her smile as they continued their witty back-and-forth.

As much as RoKo wanted to keep indulging in the conversation with AV, she found herself yawning more frequently. The exhaustion from a long day spent on her feet was catching up with her.

AV noticed too, though he was equally tired. He had spent the day riding a high—closing one of his biggest assignments and endorsements, a day filled with adrenaline and dopamine kicks. Yet, here he was, finding even more of that thrill in RoKo's presence.

He wanted to stay as much as she wanted to keep him talking, to continue stealing glances at him. But when AV checked his watch, he realized it was 4 a.m., the early morning hour known as Brahma Muhurta, a sacred time when the world begins to wake up.

They had lost all sense of time, so engrossed in each other that they hadn't even noticed the night slipping away.

It dawned on them both that while the world outside was just beginning to stir, they had yet to catch their first wink of sleep. The night had unfolded into something unexpected, a deep connection that neither had anticipated but neither was quite ready to let go of, even as the first light of dawn began to creep in.

Okay, another 15 minutes and then we'll call it a night, RoKo suggested, her voice tinged with reluctance.

AV frowned, glancing at the clock once more. Hmm, well, we'll actually have to call it a day, can't call it a night anymore. I mean, I've spent the whole night with you, well I mean talking to you, and now the dawn is breaking. Ufff, what will people think when they see me walking out of your door at this hour? he teased, with mischief in his eyes.

RoKo rolled her eyes, stifling a laugh. Seriously, AV, that's what's on your mind right now? That's your biggest worry?

Oh no, that ain't my biggest worry, AV retorted with a playful grin. My biggest worry is that there's no more water in my room, and the concierge isn't picking up.

So if I get thirsty for more, I'll have to come back to knock on your door, he added, rhyming the words together with a happy lilt in his voice.

She smiled, resisting the urge to tease him with, Yeah, as if you ever wait for my approval. Go ahead, do as you please. Instead, she played it cool, saying, Sure, why don't you take this bottle if you need it? But he shook his head, saying, No, it's fine.

He then got up, reluctantly leaving the warmth of the bed, his gaze lingering on RoKo with an intensity that made her heart skip a beat once again, once more.

As they said their goodbyes, there was an unspoken understanding between them—a subtle awareness that this might be the last time their paths would cross.

RoKo felt a deep pang in her stomach, as if she could sense the unsaid thoughts swirling in AV's mind, mirroring her own.

He walked out the door with a finality that felt almost deliberate, as if he knew this might be the last time he'd walk through it. He didn't turn back, didn't hesitate—just kept moving forward.

RoKo stood there for a moment, watching him go, a heavy feeling settling in her chest. Then, with a deep breath, she closed the door behind him, the sound of the lock clicking into place echoing in the quiet room, louder than she intended, as if sealing off a chapter she wasn't sure she was ready to end.

She didn't want him to leave, and deep down, he didn't want to go either. But if desires were rivers, they'd be swept away by the current.

AV returned to his room, heading straight into the shower, desperate to cool off both the lingering heat of RoKo's presence and the haze of the wine. The water hit his skin in heavy droplets, steaming up the small bathroom, but no matter how hot or cold he turned the tap, it couldn't wash away the pull he felt toward her. The more the water poured over him, the more it seemed to fuel the fire she had ignited inside him, clinging to his skin like a stubborn memory.

Frustrated, he stepped out, toweling off quickly before slipping into his T-shirt and shorts. Yet, even as he dressed, the thought of her stayed, tugging at him, relentless. He tried to push it aside, but it was no use. Less than 20 minutes later, he found himself once again standing outside her door, knocking for the third time, as though some unseen force had drawn him back, unable to break free from the gravity of her existence.

RoKo, having taken a power nap, wasn't expecting him. She was anticipating the housekeeping staff delivering the water bottles she had requested. But when she opened the door, there stood AV, looking even more striking than before—his body-hugging T-shirt clinging to his broad chest, highlighting every sculpted muscle. His legs, strong and toned beneath his shorts, and his short hair still damp from the shower, glistening with water. The sight of him, almost dripping wet and impossibly handsome, felt surreal, almost as if she were still dreaming.

A thousand thoughts raced through her mind as she took in the sight before her. His casual attire somehow only amplified his presence, and the fresh, clean scent mixed with the intensity in his eyes sent her pulse into overdrive.

As AV stepped into the room without a word, the boundaries of friendship and something more were almost beginning to blur.

RoKo could feel her pulse quicken as she realized that whatever was unfolding between them was beyond their control, something neither of them could resist, nor wanted to.

Hey, I need some water, he said, his voice low. I told you I might come back if I needed it, and here I am. You hoarder! Just look at the number of bottles in your room—and I'm not even counting the empty ones.

But now that I'm here, and it's early morning, how about I whip up a cup of coffee for both of us? Did you know a shot of coffee right before bed can actually help you sleep better? You can say thank you for the insight I just shared! He grinned. And yeah, after that, we can finally retreat to our respective beds and call it a day... or night. Don't worry, this time, it won't be your bed. You can snuggle up in your own, and I'll deliver the coffee like a personal butler.

He paused, his eyes locked onto hers, a hint of something deeper in his gaze. May I have the pleasure of making you a coffee, Madam RoKo? he asked, his tone softening, almost reverent.

This time, he didn't rush—he waited, letting the question stay and persist in the air between them, hoping she would say yes, savouring the anticipation of her answer.

RoKo hesitated for a moment, feeling the weight of his gaze, the underlying current of something more than just a simple offer of coffee. There was a spark of warm glimmer in his eyes, but also a sincerity that made her heart skip a beat.

Well, since you put it so charmingly... how can I refuse? she finally said, a smile curling on her lips and a groggy demeanour.

AV's grin widened, the room suddenly feeling a bit smaller, more intimate. Perfect. Let me show you my coffee-making skills—though I have to warn you, they might just be as intoxicating as the wine.

With that, he moved toward the kitchenette, his movements deliberate, almost as if he were performing a ritual, the air buzzing with a thrill, charged with a power and momentum that could lead them somewhere entirely unexpected.

He looked even more captivating and irresistible in this casual avatar, his presence drawing her in like a moth to a flame. RoKo could hardly take her eyes off him, her casual glances quickly turning into deep, lingering stares.

AV, noticing her gaze, smiled to himself before meeting her eyes.

If you keep looking at me like this, he teased, you might just fall in love with me.

Without missing a beat, he began to softly sing an old Hindi song, his voice rich and warm, filling the room with a nostalgic melody:

Aisa na mujhe tum dekho, Seeney se laga lunga, Tumko main chura lunga tumsa, apna bana lun ga....

The way he sang, with such ease and affection, sent a warm thrill through her.

Armaan was undeniably handsome—the kind of man who could turn heads without even trying.

If he had chosen to pursue a career in modelling, he could have easily become a runway sensation, and in Bollywood, he would have effortlessly carved out his own space. There was something almost cinematic about him, a blend of Hritik Roshan's sharp features and Akshay Kumar's rugged charm, all wrapped up in a towering 6'2" frame.

RoKo found herself in a state of awe, still trying to grasp the surreal reality of what had unfolded between them so far and excited for more. How could this be happening? It felt like a dream, one where someone as extraordinary as Armaan was within arm's reach.

Not that RoKo was any less of a charmer herself—at 5'7 , with curly brown hair that seemed to have a life of its own, deep brown eyes that held a world of secrets, and a figure that was both graceful and elegant, perhaps with a touch of softness. But it was this very softness that added to her allure, a warmth that was impossible to ignore.

Their proximity was almost electric, a subtle current that made the air between them hum and RoKo couldn't help but marvel at the situation, wondering if fate was playing a deliciously ironic game with her.

Thinking of the endless possibilities of where this could lead, they had spent a night together—or rather, an evening that seamlessly flowed into a night—in each other's presence, sharing moments both conscious and unconscious of their significance. RoKo couldn't take her eyes off Armaan as he effortlessly whipped up an aromatic cup of coffee.

The scene felt almost too perfect, like something out of a movie, and yet there she was, living it. But just as she was about to lose herself in the moment, something unexpected happened.

Out of nowhere and out of nothing, RoKo had a sudden, vivid hallucination. It was as if one of those wise butterflies—the ones that always seemed to flutter in her anxiety-filled tummy—had materialized right in front of her, staring her down with an intensity that sent chills up her spine.

This butterfly wasn't just a figment of her imagination; it was almost flesh and blood, confronting her with a stern look.

What are you even thinking? the butterfly seemed to ask, its voice sharp and full of concern.

This is not the direction you want to head. Do you realize you've made this mistake so many times before?

You open up like the moon, fall in love too soon, then nurse your heartbreak, till it plays the same tune—dragging on for months, maybe even years. Haven't you learned anything out of it by now?

The butterfly knew RoKo well—and often spoke in the language of logic and strategy. But this was different. This was personal, and the butterfly was here to set her straight.

With a swift, almost magical gesture, the butterfly seemed to tap RoKo with a wand, as if it were an angel trying to wake her up from a dangerous dream. RoKo, wake up. This is not for you!

The butterfly's voice was filled with urgency. You don't realize it yet, but he's not real—not in the way you're imagining him to be. You don't love him, RoKo. You're just in awe of him because you see him as another version of yourself, you see him as Another You, a reflection of everything you aspire to be. He's a well-refined, well-defined male version of you, and that's what's drawing you in. This is infatuation, not love. You're getting attached because he embodies all the qualities you admire, but that doesn't make it real.

The wise butterfly's warning hit hard, echoing in RoKo's mind.

I'm cautioning you, because if your heart breaks again, don't come calling out to me. I'm tired, RoKo. I'm literally giving up on you.

While RoKo was still immersed in the wise butterfly's words of caution, reflecting deeply on the sudden shift in her emotions, Armaan's voice jolted her back to reality.

Tadaaaa! Here's your hot cup of the world's best coffee, Madam! But hey, where are you lost again? Feeling sleepy? Trust me, this coffee will give you the best wake-up call! Armaan grinned, before adding with a childlike innocence to his lovely smile, And hey, Armaan does make a delicious one, trust me on that. Everyone says so—from Japan to Russia! He smiled, the innocence of a child shining through, making it impossible for RoKo not to smile back.

RoKo smiled faintly, her mind still echoing with the butterfly's warning. She whispered to herself, Yeah, I just got a wake-up call, and now it's time to really wake up.

Thank you, Armaan, she said aloud, taking the cup from him. This is amazing... and a little strange, too—first wine late into the night, and now coffee at dawn with a stranger. She felt a subtle shift within herself, growing distant from the bubbling energy that had flowed between them just moments ago. Her thoughts were spiralling, trying to make sense of what this all meant.

Hey, hey! Armaan's voice cut through RoKo's deepening thoughts, pulling her back to the present. He could sense the shift in her mood, the seriousness that was beginning to cloud her expression. With a light-hearted tone, he continued, We're no longer strangers, remember? We're two people who were strangers, but now... what can I call us? Friends? Maybe even partners in crime for a few hours.

We're two souls who just collided in the most unexpected of ways. Maybe even accomplices in this little adventure we've found ourselves in.

His eyes sparkled with mischief as he leaned in a little closer. "So, we've had a One Wine Stand, a One Water Bottle Stand, and now a One Coffee Stand," he said, his grin widening. "Seems like we've summed up our very own One Night Stand!" he added, bursting into laughter, clearly enjoying his own cleverness

His laughter was infectious, a sound so genuine and carefree that it broke through RoKo's inner turmoil, pulling a reluctant smile from her as well. The look in his eyes was impossible to resist, making the moment feel lighter, almost as if they were in on a secret that only they understood.

As the laughter faded, RoKo found herself staring into the coffee Armaan had just handed her, the rich aroma mingling with the lingering sense of unease left behind by the butterfly's words. The warmth of the cup in her hands contrasted sharply with the cold clarity of her thoughts, making her wonder if this brief encounter was something to savor—or something she needed to step away from before it turned into another chapter in her long history of heartbreaks.

Was it just a hallucination, or was it a wake-up call from her own subconscious, urging her to tread carefully?

The questions hung in the air, unanswered, as she watched Armaan, feeling both drawn to him and suddenly, inexplicably distant. In that brief silence, she realized the fine line she was walking—torn between the intoxicating charm of the moment and the need to protect herself from yet another potential heartache.

But why the heck do you think you'll end up with heartbreak or heartache? the 999 butterflies knocked in unison, their voices circling in RoKo's mind like a gentle yet insistent breeze.

Since when did you start sounding so negative? Why can't you just live in the moment, savor the sweetness of it, and make memories that will sparkle in your mind like stars in the night sky?

This isn't your moment of truth, after all. It's not like he's proposed—has he? So why are you casting shadows over a future that might never even exist under these conditions?

This might be the last time you see him, or it could be the very first chapter of something new. But you haven't even turned the page yet, and already you're thinking about closing the book?

Think about all the times you've thrown yourself headfirst into love, with all your heart, all your spirit—weren't those moments worth it, even if they ended in heartbreak?

Those people who have loved you, even for a transient moment, carry the memory of how you made them feel. So stop trying to read the last page before you've even written the first line.

Come back to the present. Immerse yourself in it, really feel it, and hold on for as long as it lasts. Because nothing stays the same forever. People change, feelings fade, and circumstances shift. Everything has a shelf life, no matter how perfect it feels in the moment. So stay here, in this moment, before it slips away.

Neither you nor Armaan will remain the same forever. And if, one day, he does break your heart, or you break his—so what? That's the nature of life. We're sure that neither of you would do it with the intent to hurt each other. You're both more than that.

The butterflies' words fluttered through her mind like a whispered secret, a sigh of relief that softened the edges of her anxiety.

It felt as though RoKo had received the permission she didn't even know she needed—permission to let go, to lower her guard, and to be her vulnerable, authentic self. Go ahead, they seemed to say, open up, laugh, share your stories. Have a good conversation. He won't judge you, and even if he does, it won't matter.

You don't have to spend your life with him or love him forever. You can always move on—move on with grace, with dignity, just as you've always done. After all, you're not some lovestruck teenager; you're a mature woman who knows how to navigate the tides of life.

With that, RoKo felt a calmness settle over her, as if the storm of doubts had passed, leaving behind a clear, tranquil sky. She decided to let herself be present, to enjoy the moment without worrying about the paths it might or might not lead to.

She would allow herself to drift in the current of the now, letting the future unfold as it wished, without trying to force it into any particular shape.

Guess I'm having my coffee all by myself, Armaan remarked, his tone light, though something deeper lurked beneath.

Why do I feel like you're here but not really here, RoKo? Did I say something wrong? Did I make you uncomfortable? Are you okay? Armaan wondered in his mind.

He paused, watching her from the corner of his eye. He couldn't quite put his finger on it, but something felt different. There was a distance now, a gap he hadn't noticed before. We were getting there, he thought. Sharing laughs, wine, coffee... even those random moments with Wrigleys and water bottles. But now? Now, there was only silence. It wasn't supposed to feel like this.

Earlier, I thought you were just a stranger, then maybe a friend, and later, perhaps someone I was meant to meet. But now... it feels like nothing but silence.

He cleared his throat, trying to mask the unease in his chest. If you're tired, we can call it a day, he said gently, his voice carrying the concern he couldn't quite express. Should we?

The concern in Armaan's voice tugged at RoKo, pulling her out of the fog of her overthinking. She realized that in her worry about the future, she had momentarily lost sight of the present—of the effortless connection they were building, one playful moment at a time.

No, no, I'm okay, she replied, shaking off her thoughts and forcing a smile. Just got lost in my head for a minute there. Didn't mean to make things awkward. I'm really enjoying this time with you, Armaan.

Her words seemed to reassure him, the strain in his shoulders easing as he leaned back in his chair. Good, he said, his smile returning. Because I'd hate to think we were losing that vibe we had going. But if you're tired, really, we can pick this up another time. Or we can stay up a little longer, see where the conversation takes us—no pressure.

RoKo looked at him, feeling the warmth of his presence slowly melting away the last of her doubts. Let's keep going, she said, her voice steadying. I think there's still some more coffee—and maybe a few more laughs—left in us tonight—or should I say morning? No, wait, early morning, when even time feels a little confused.

The night had already worn out and the weight of the day had begun to settle in, yet neither RoKo nor Armaan was ready to let go of the moment. The wine left its mark on their tongues, the coffee added a sharp contrast, and the exhaustion from the previous day's long hours weighed heavily, threatening to take over.

But there was something about this connection—something elusive, just beyond their grasp—that made them want to stretch the moment as far as it could go.

RoKo's mind was a flurry of thoughts and emotions, her butterflies whirling around like they were late to a party, each one representing a different fear, a different hope. And while RoKo had her butterflies, Armaan had Froggy. Froggy wasn't just any childhood toy; he was Armaan's trusted sidekick, the quiet voice of reason that had steered him through countless decisions. Now, with the night giving way to morning, the sunrise about to steal the show, and everything feeling strangely high-stakes, Froggy, ever the opportunist, decided to make his grand entrance.

Armaan, buddy, Froggy's voice echoed in his mind, what exactly are you doing? You've had your fun, sure, but where is this going? You've got that big presentation at 10 a.m., and here you are, getting lost in a moment that might not even mean anything tomorrow. This isn't like you—underslept, tipsy, and flirting with the idea of throwing it all away for what? A few laughs, a few drinks, and maybe a little thrill?

Armaan tried to shake Froggy's concerns, but the voice was relentless. You're not like her, Armaan. You've always been the steady one, the planner, meticulous and grounded, the guy who thinks things through. She's impulsive, spontaneous, and sure, that's attractive right now, but what about tomorrow? Who lets a stranger into their room, drinks wine with them, and talks all night like this? She's not the one for you, Armaan. You've got to think long-term, not just about tonight. This is not sustainable and you know it, You know yourself Armaan!!

Armaan frowned slightly, trying to reason with the voice in his head. Froggy, you're being too judgmental. I'm the one who initiated this. I knocked on her door, not the other way around. I invited myself in her life. And did you even take a brief moment to see her tonight? She's got something—a spark, a kind of fearless energy, more like spitfire energy—and that's rare. She walked into that room full of men not a hint of hesitation, completely owning the space, commanding it with an air of power. That's not recklessness—that's confidence. And that's what drew me in.

But Froggy wasn't about to back down. Confidence or recklessness? Think about it, Armaan. What kind of woman does that? Either she's oblivious to the dangers, or she's deliberately playing a risky game. And you? What are you really after here? Is this just the wine talking, or are you starting to wonder if there's something between the two of you, huh?

Armaan's mind raced as he searched for the right words. No, Froggy, you've got it wrong. If she was just after some fling, she'd be in bed with me right now. But she's not. We're here, talking, connecting on a level that goes beyond the physical. And don't hit me with that tired line about men and women not being able to be just friends. We're more than capable of that—or at least, I'd like to believe we are.

Despite his internal arguments, Armaan couldn't deny that Froggy's words had struck a chord. The moment felt charged, electric and as much as he wanted to stay in control, a part of him was already slipping, caught up in the gravitational pull that RoKo seemed to have on him.

Armaan could sense it, an unspoken bond pulling them together and pulling him even closer in the moment inspite of Froggy urging him to step back, he realized that whatever was unfolding between them, it wasn't something he could just walk away from—not yet, anyway.

He looked over at RoKo, who was lost in her own thoughts, her eyes distant as if she too was wrestling with her own inner voices.

The room was filled with a quiet understanding; they didn't need to fill the space with words. Just being in each other's presence was enough, the air around them humming with unspoken thoughts.

Armaan didn't know where this was going, or what it meant, but he knew one thing for certain—he wasn't ready to end the night just yet. Not when the possibility of something was still floating afresh in the air, just waiting to be explored.

Hey, do you need a refill on that coffee? Or... Armaan leaned in slightly, his smirk widening. Maybe just a little more of me?

What? RoKo shot back, raising an eyebrow.

I meant, coffee, obviously! Armaan grinned, throwing in an exaggerated wink. But hey, Madam RoKo, feel free to command some wine too, if that's more your style. Your wish is my command! He flourished his hand dramatically, his playful tone turning the quiet moment into a mini performance.

RoKo chuckled, her eyes sparkling as she caught onto his tease. Smooth, AV, she replied, using his initials in that familiar way she'd adopted. But no, not really. I have this review with my boss at 8 a.m., and my head's already doing somersaults. Not sure how I'm going to pull through.

Armaan's expression shifted to one of genuine concern. Well, in that case, allow me to offer two solutions: first, a foolproof remedy to dodge that looming hangover u feeling is starting to build up, and second, I can tuck you into bed if you don't mind! he said, his tone light but earnest.

RoKo raised an eyebrow, feigning offense. Tuck me in? Seriously, Armaan? I'm not a baby, she quipped, crossing her arms with mock indignation.

Oh, trust me, you're way worse than one, RoKo! he fired back, grinning wickedly. But, really, I insist. Let me help—it's the absolute least I can do after dragging you into this late-night chaos. He gave a mock bow, as if offering some grand gesture, his eyes twinkling with mischief.

She rolled her eyes, but the smile tugging at her lips betrayed her. The mix of exhaustion and the fading warmth of the wine dulled any will to protest. Alright, Doctor AV, she sighed, throwing her hands up in mock surrender. Do your worst Doc.

Armaan sprang into action, disappearing briefly and returning with a small packet. Baking soda, he announced triumphantly, mixing it into a glass of water and handing it to her. Works like magic against hangovers. Trust me, I've saved many lives with this concoction.

Looks like you're someone who's quite familiar with hangovers, RoKo remarked, one eyebrow raised skeptically as she held her drink.

Well, if not me, then at least my friends are, Armaan laughed, the sound rich and full in the quiet room. But you're right—I've certainly played guardian angel to my fair share of friends. And tonight, you're one of them. So instead of throwing sarcasm my way, maybe you could show a little gratitude for coming to your rescue before your 8 a.m. meeting.

If you're really in the mood to throw something, just make sure it's not in the bathroom, he quipped with a grin. Anything else you toss my way, I'll handle with grace. After all, I've played national-level cricket and state-level football—so you can imagine, dodging curveballs is my thing.

She laughed, taking a tentative sip and grimacing at the taste. Fine, fine. Thank you, oh wise one. This better work, or my boss will be coming after me.

Alright, now for part two of my master plan. Let's get you tucked in so you can catch some proper sleep.

RoKo smirked, her eyes dancing with amusement. You really take this caretaking role seriously, don't you? Do you offer bedtime stories too?

Only on special request, Armaan quipped, as he carefully pulled the blanket over her. RoKo looked up at him, you seem awfully good at this. Looks like you have quite a bit of experience tucking people in—maybe lot of them? she teased, her tone laced with gentle sarcasm.

Armaan met her gaze, his expression intense but still warm. If you've got something to say, be a straight shooter. If you want to ask me something, just ask it, he replied, his voice low but steady. But let's get one thing clear—no, I don't make a habit of knocking on hotel doors in the middle of the night, sharing wine, or tucking people into bed. What happened tonight.... even I'm still trying to wrap my head around it. So, before you go pointing fingers, maybe hold off on the judgment. You're accusing me of something I haven't done, while you—his eyes narrowed slightly—were in a room full of drunk men. Now, that's a bit callous, don't you think?

RoKo raised an eyebrow, a bit taken aback by his candidness. Oh, that's quite a comeback, Armaan, she retorted, though she couldn't help but feel a twinge of admiration for his honesty.

Hey, I'm just giving you a taste of your own medicine—or wait, no, wine, he said, his voice lightening. Oh wait, wait, it was me who brought both the medicine and the wine!

Okay, whatever, she replied, rolling her eyes but unable to suppress a smile.

Armaan's expression softened as he continued, Let's just say I was raised to take care of the people I care about. And right now, that includes you. By the way, is this how you want to say goodnight? His voice had a hint of something deeper, something that made RoKo's heart the faintest skip.

No, not at all. I don't want to, RoKo admitted, her voice barely above a whisper.

Neither do I, Armaan replied, Now, close those eyes and get some rest. You've got a big day ahead, and I won't have you blaming me for any underperformance.

She found herself momentarily speechless. She laughed softly, her eyelids already growing heavy. No promises, but I'll try my best. Goodnight, Armaan.

Goodnight, he whispered, his voice gentle as he brushed a stray strand of hair away from her forehead. For a moment, he paused, observing the peacefulness that had settled over her features.

Quietly, Armaan set about tidying up the room, collecting the empty wine glasses and discarded wrappers. He moved with practiced ease, ensuring everything was in its rightful place before turning off the lights, leaving only the soft glow of the city lights filtering through the curtains.

As he reached the door, he cast one last glance back at RoKo, now almost peacefully asleep. A soft smile touched his lips as he whispered to himself, Sleep well, mystery girl. Until next time. With that, he slipped out into the hallway, the door clicking softly behind him.

Walking back to his own room, Armaan felt a mix of emotions swirling within him. There was a lightness, a sense of contentment he hadn't felt in a long time, mingled with curiosity and anticipation for what the morning might bring. Despite the late hour and the important presentation looming ahead, he couldn't suppress the smile that refused to fade as he prepared for bed, thoughts of RoKo drifting through his mind like a pleasant dream.

Little did they both know, this was just the beginning of a story neither had expected but perhaps both secretly hoped for.

Though Armaan had returned to his room, an unusual sense of loneliness settled over him. The excitement and thrill of the night had faded, leaving behind a simmering confusion. He had enjoyed his mysterious company far more than he had expected, and now he found himself in a daze, questioning how he could have let himself get so carried away.

This wasn't like him. Armaan had always been a man who valued his reputation and dignity above all else—never one to act impulsively or recklessly. He prided himself on being grounded, on having control, on ensuring that every step he took was measured and thoughtful.

Yet here he was, replaying the night in his mind, and every time he tried to rationalize it, a voice inside him whispered,

What if? What if someone had seen him leaving her room in the early morning hours? What if they judged him? He was the type who would have raised an eyebrow if a friend had shared a similar story—wine and conversation alone, really? So how could he expect others to believe it? Not that he would share this story with anyone, but the thought of the 'what ifs' stared him right in the face, tearing at his peace and leaving him uneasy.

As these thoughts churned in his mind, Froggy, his ever-present inner voice, made a sudden reappearance. Froggy had been with him for years, a companion that had always guided him with a mix of logic and sarcasm, never shy to pull him back to reality.

Yes, you're absolutely right, Froggy chimed in, his tone tinged with a mix of concern and exasperation. This is exactly what I was trying to tell you back in that room. This isn't you. It's as if you were overpowered by some spirit. I just hope this mystery girl of yours—what's her name huh, oh right yeah, RoKo?—isn't into hypnosis or something. Armaan, you need to snap out of it. I need my Armaan back. Get out of these looping thoughts about Madame and get back to reality.

Armaan sighed, running a hand through his hair. Hey, Froggy, you know I haven't caught a wink all night give me a break! His voice carried a blend of exhaustion and frustration, as if pleading with Froggy to cut him some slack for once.

So be it, Armaan, Froggy insisted, unyielding. Get to the gym, get that dopamine flowing. Work out the last remnants of this haze. Then, come back, polish off the final touches of your presentation, shower up again, have a hearty healthy breakfast, and be ready to put on the Armaan show with poise and charm.

Froggy's voice softened, but the urgency remained, The past is over, Armaan. This is your now, and in your now, Madame RoKo is not a part of the plan. So can we focus and do what we need to do?

Armaan felt the weight of Froggy's words settle in, grounding him back to the reality he had temporarily escaped. He knew Froggy was right. The night had been a departure from who he was, a brief detour into an unfamiliar territory that had left him feeling feeling a bit disoriented. But he was Armaan, after all—strong, ambitious, principled, and focused. He couldn't let a short lived moment, no matter how enticing, derail him from the path he had worked so hard to carve out for himself.

With a deep breath, he stood up, shaking off the remnants of the night like dust from his shoulders. He had a mission, a purpose, and he needed to reclaim that focus. He glanced in the mirror, seeing the resolve harden in his eyes. It was time to leave behind the echoes of the past hours and step back into the man he knew himself to be. It was time to hit the gym and get his old self back in the now.

Armaan moved with purpose, grabbing his gym bag and tossing in his essentials. Froggy's words still echoed in his mind, firm yet reassuring. The past is over. This is your now. He pulled on his workout gear, the comfortable stretch of the fabric a reminder of countless mornings spent just like this, focused and ready to crush his goals. He needed this. He needed to sweat it all out and reset.

Armaan entered the gym, the familiar buzz of energy already working its way into his system. The smell of rubber mats and metal weights grounded him, a stark contrast to the haze of thoughts he'd been trying to shake off. He scanned the room, nodding to a few early risers. This was his place, where focus wasn't just a goal but a given.

His workout playlist kicked in as he secured his earbuds. Alright, let's do this. He headed for the treadmill, ready to warm up.

He started with a 5-minute jog on the treadmill, easing into the motion. His muscles responded as he picked up the pace, the steady rhythm of his feet hitting the belt syncing with the beat in his ears. Get the blood flowing, shake off the night.

His mind wandered briefly to the conversation with Froggy. Stay in the now, Armaan. He increased the speed slightly before stepping off, feeling his body come to life.

Next, he moved to the squat rack. Time to get serious. He loaded the bar and began his first set of squats, feeling the familiar strain in his legs. Four sets, twelve reps each. The weight was heavy, but not unbearable. Each movement felt like a reminder of control, focus, and strength. This is what you're good at. But even as he pushed through the reps, a flicker of RoKo's smile crept into his thoughts. He shook his head, focusing back on the task at hand. One rep at a time.

From there, it was straight to deadlifts—four sets, ten reps. The weight felt solid in his hands, the bar pressing against his palms as he lifted. He loved the feeling of the bar pulling him down and his body pulling it right back up. Control the weight, control your thoughts. But as the set went on, his mind betrayed him. RoKo. The way she'd laughed last night. He tightened his grip on the bar. Focus. Froggy's right—this is your time.

Armaan shifted to the bench press next, lying flat beneath the bar, the weight above him. Four sets, eight reps. His muscles worked hard, chest burning with each lift. This is where you reclaim your focus, he reminded himself. But the ease of last night's conversation, the way they connected, kept slipping through his focus like water through his fingers. Was it just the wine?

Next were pull-ups, three sets of ten reps. Hanging from the bar, he exhaled sharply, the tension in his shoulders mirroring the internal tug-of-war in his mind. Each pull was a battle between wanting to leave last night behind and being stuck in the what-ifs. She wasn't supposed to linger this long in my thoughts. But here he was, stuck in the same loop as he powered through the last set.

Moving on to shoulder presses, he felt the weight bear down on him, three sets of ten reps. This is your space. Stay focused. The voice of Froggy echoed in his mind, trying to pull him back to the present. RoKo's not part of the plan. Focus, Armaan. Yet, no matter how hard he tried, the memory of her laughter during the ramp walk kept sneaking back.

He could still see her doubled over, giggling at his exaggerated catwalk moves, teasing him with mock applause as if he were strutting down a fashion runway. Each time he pushed the weights up, the echo of her voice crept into his thoughts: "You're practically a model, AV!" The more he tried to focus, the more her laughter replayed, making him want to chuckle mid-set. How am I supposed to focus with her dancing around in my brain? he thought, fighting back a smirk.

He finished with planks, three sets of 90 seconds. His core burned as he held the position, arms shaking slightly as the seconds ticked by. She can't take over this much space in your head, he told himself, but the truth was harder to ignore with every passing moment. Can someone really make that much of an impact in such a short time?

The workout ended with a cooldown stretch—seven minutes of loosening his muscles. His body felt good, but his mind was still restless. It's just the aftermath of the night, he reasoned. By the time I'm done with my presentation, this will all be a faint memory. Yet, as he reached for his toes, a small voice whispered in the back of his mind: But will it? No matter how hard he tried, the thought of her kept creeping in, refusing to be dismissed so easily.

But as he stretched his arms overhead, RoKo's smile flashed in his mind once more. He let out a small, frustrated sigh, knowing deep down that no matter how many sets he did or how much focus he tried to reclaim, something had shifted. She wasn't a part of the plan, but that didn't mean she hadn't left her mark. In fact, it felt like she had carved out a space in his thoughts, one he couldn't quite push away.

Armaan stood, towel draped over his shoulder, muscles aching but alive. He'd done the workout, gone through the motions, but his mind was still racing. Each rep had pushed his body, but his thoughts had never quite escaped her. Fine, he thought, as he headed for the locker room. Maybe she wasn't a part of the plan. But plans change...

FOUR

THE NEXT MORNING OR DAY AS WE MAY CALL IT!!!

As RoKo stirred awake, the remnants of the previous night clung to her like a stubborn fog. The late-night conversation with AV, which had felt so intoxicatingly profound at the time, had stretched into the early hours, ending only at 5:30 a.m.

The dialogue had been deep, layered with subtle connections and unspoken emotions, but now, in the unforgiving light of morning, it left her with a pounding headache and a sense of disarray.

She hadn't intended to stay up that late—she hadn't intended for any of it, really. But there was something about AV, something that had kept her tethered to that moment, unwilling to let it slip away.

RoKo groaned as she reached for her phone, its screen glaring back at her with the harsh reminder of her first call of the day, scheduled for 8 a.m.

Barely two hours of sleep, and she was supposed to be sharp, focused, and ready to tackle the day with her usual vigor. Instead, she felt groggy, her head heavy as if it were stuffed with cotton, and the fading effects of last night's wine mingled with the unmistakable weight of a hangover, though slightly eased by the concoction AV made for her.

As she glanced at the clock, she realized she had little choice but to push through the haze. The world wasn't going to wait for her to catch up, and there were expectations to meet.

She lay there for a moment, the events of the night playing on a loop in her mind. The way AV's voice had softened when he spoke her name, the way his eyes had seemed to see right through her. And then, as if mocking her, that wise butterfly fluttered back into her thoughts, whispering warnings she was too tired to heed. What had she done? What had she been thinking? But the memory of AV's laugh, rich and full, pushed those thoughts aside, at least for now.

With a deep sigh, RoKo pushed herself up, wincing as the room seemed to tilt slightly, the after effects of the wine making their presence known. She needed to pull herself together, needed to shake off this feeling and face the day. But as she looked at the clock again, she couldn't help but wish for just a few more minutes in the cocoon of her bed, away from the world, away from the complexities of her feelings, and away from the memory of AV that seemed to linger in the very air around her.

But reality was knocking at her door, demanding her attention. She forced herself to her feet, knowing that today was not going to wait for her to sort out the mess in her head. She had to be RoKo—the strong, confident woman who handled her business unit and P&L with grace and poise. Yet, as she splashed cold water on her face, she couldn't shake the thought of AV, couldn't shake the feeling that something had changed between them, something she wasn't quite ready to define.

The hangover was bad—one of the worst she'd had in a while. She blamed it partly on the wine she'd sipped during the conversation with AV, but even more so on the emotional rollercoaster she'd been on since meeting him. The combination left her feeling off-kilter, like she was moving through a fog that refused to lift, every step heavy with the weight of her own thoughts.

As she settled back into her pillows, phone in hand, RoKo decided to take her first call of the day right from bed. It was supposed to be a simple update—just a routine check-in, something she could handle even in her current state. But as the call connected, she realized how deeply the grogginess had sunk into her bones. Her words felt sluggish, like they were moving through molasses, and her mind struggled to keep up with the conversation. Each response felt delayed, as if her brain had to wade through the fog before finding the right words.

She could feel the tension building behind her eyes, the tell-tale sign of a headache that was only going to get worse. The day had barely begun, but already it was demanding more from her than she felt capable of giving. The weight of it all pressed down on her, making her wish she could hit pause, rewind to a time before last night, before everything had gotten so complicated. But there was no going back, only forward, and RoKo knew she had to push through—somehow, she had to find the strength to face whatever the day had in store.

As she got onto her email account to get started, there came an email and then another one and then another one, the day had begun, the inflow had started pouring in and then came THE email—a terse, passive-aggressive message from her dotted-line manager. It wasn't the first time he'd tried to exert control over her travel arrangements, demanding to know where and when she would be traveling, despite the fact that she didn't report directly to him. But this morning, it felt like the final straw. The

P&L she managed wasn't even under his purview, yet he acted as if it was his right to dictate her every move.

The power struggle had been simmering for months, but today it almost reached its breaking point. RoKo could feel her patience fraying, her usual calm slipping away. It wasn't just the hangover, or the lack of sleep, or even the emotionally charged conversation with AV. It was the sheer exhaustion of constantly having to defend her autonomy, her decisions, her right to lead without unnecessary interference.

She took a deep breath, trying to steady herself, but the frustration was already bubbling to the surface. How had it come to this? How had she ended up here, battling for control over something that should have been hers to manage freely? The whole situation felt absurd, like a game she had no interest in playing, yet was forced to participate in.

As she read through the email, the words seemed to blur together, fuelled by her mounting anger. The unnecessary pettiness of it all eroded her patience, pushing her closer to the edge. She had worked too hard, fought too many battles, to be undermined like this. The morning had already begun on a sour note, and this was just the tipping point.

Her fingers hovered over the keypad, trembling with the urge to respond immediately, to fire back a pointed reply that would put him in his place. But she stopped herself, taking another deep breath. This wasn't the time to act impulsively, no matter how justified her anger felt. Instead, she needed to channel that frustration into something productive, to reclaim the control she was so fiercely fighting for.

The day stretched out before her like a long, uphill climb, and RoKo knew she'd need to summon every ounce of strength she had left to get through it. But as she sat there, staring at her phone, her thoughts kept drifting back to AV (time and again, time and again, in a never ending loop)—how their conversation had shifted something inside her, how it had opened up a space she hadn't known existed.

This felt like the beginning of something extraordinary, she realized—not just with AV, but within herself. It was a beginning that demanded she face these challenges head-on, that she confront the power struggles, the exhaustion, the emotional hangovers, and come out stronger on the other side. But right now, all she wanted was another hour of sleep.

She sighed, pushing herself up from the bed once again, knowing well that there were calls to take, emails to answer, and battles to fight. But beneath it all, there was also a new awareness—a sense that something was shifting, something profound and necessary.

It was the start of a journey she couldn't fully understand yet, but one that she knew she couldn't avoid. Whatever lay ahead, she would face it, groggy and hungover perhaps, but with a new sense of purpose slowly emerging from the fog. And maybe, just maybe, she wouldn't have to face it alone.

Her thoughts drifted back to the night before. It had been one of those rare, serendipitous evenings where two strangers find themselves sharing more than just pleasantries.

By the time they said their goodbyes at 5:30 a.m., they weren't strangers anymore. The night had stretched on, each hour peeling back layers of conversation until they found themselves not just talking, but actually seeing each other. They knew a bit about each other—maybe even more than they had planned to share. But, of course, they had only shown the best parts of themselves, the sides they were proud of, while carefully keeping the rougher edges hidden.

Isn't that what everyone does when meeting someone new? You protect your vulnerabilities, showing only the shiny, polished sides, hoping the other person will be impressed. But even as they talked, there was an unspoken understanding between them—a sense that there were deeper layers they weren't ready to reveal. It was in the pauses between their words, in the glances that lingered a little too long, and in the way their laughter sometimes felt like it was covering up something deeper.

This unspoken connection made RoKo pause, replaying the moments in her mind, wondering if they had both glimpsed what lay beneath the surface, even if they weren't ready to talk about it yet. Had their carefully guarded facades cracked just enough for the other to see through? And if they had, what had they seen?

There was an odd comfort in thinking that they might both be carrying their own hidden feelings, acknowledged but not spoken aloud —feelings shaped by past traumas that still cast shadows over their present. But at the same time, there was uncertainty about what those hidden feelings really were—shared vulnerabilities or things better left unsaid?

But as dawn broke, the moment passed. The unspoken remained unspoken, the deeper layers stayed hidden, and they went their separate ways, leaving behind the unresolved question of what might have happened if only they had dared to reveal a bit more, if they had let their hearts truly pour, for they were strangers at the core, free from judgment, with nothing to fear for sure.

RoKo had quietly wondered if AV might knock on her door again this morning or perhaps call to suggest breakfast. After all, last night had meant something, hadn't it?

Something that felt significant, even if it was under the influence of a few too many drinks.

As she sat in her bed, the early morning light filtering through the curtains, replaying the moments in her mind—the way their conversation had flowed effortlessly, she couldn't help but smile.

But as the hours ticked by, the room remained silent. There was no knock on the door, no call, not even a text. She kept glancing at her phone, waiting for it to light up with his name, her anticipation slowly turning into a sinking feeling of doubt.

Each minute that passed felt like an eternity, the silence growing louder, more oppressive. She tried to brush it off, telling herself that maybe he was just busy, maybe he had overslept, or maybe he was giving her space. Yet, with each passing minute, the hope she had felt began to wane, replaced by a creeping sense of reality.

The reality that perhaps she had misread the signs, that maybe what felt like a connection was just a momentary spark in the haze of the night. Eventually, unable to bear the silence any longer, she reached out to him.

Her message was casual, breezy—just a suggestion to meet for breakfast if he had the time. She typed it out quickly, trying not to overthink it, trying to keep the tone light, as if it didn't really matter. But when his reply came, it was polite but curt, the kind of response that left no room for further conversation.

An important meeting, he had said, something he couldn't reschedule. It was the kind of excuse that felt all too familiar, the kind that was meant to let someone down gently without actually saying it outright.

Well, she thought, *I guess last night didn't mean much to him after all.* The realization hit her with a dull thud, the excitement and connection she had felt now seeming almost foolish in the light of day.

She felt a pang of disappointment, a small ache in her chest as the fantasy she had begun to build unravelled before her eyes. Maybe it was just the alcohol talking, she mused—those drinks softening the edges, lowering walls and inhibitions, making two people feel closer than they truly were

She sighed, pushing the thoughts aside, trying to convince herself that it was better this way. Better to let it go now, before she got too invested, before the disappointment could sink its claws any deeper. After all, she had been here before—*getting too caught up in a moment, only to find out that it meant little to the other person.*

Did she feel bad about it? Maybe for a passing moment, but just as quickly as the emotion came, it washed away, like footprints in the sand swept clean by the next wave. The high tide of disappointment ebbed into a low tide of indifference, leaving behind a quiet shoreline, undisturbed and calm.

The storm that once stirred her heart had passed, leaving no trace. The connection she'd imagined, once a bright spark, now felt like a brief flicker, dimming as quickly as it ignited. What once seemed urgent now felt distant, blurry, and insubstantial.

The world hadn't shifted on its axis after all; it had simply carried on, as it always did, indifferent to the transient emotions of the people within it.

RoKo smiled to herself, a knowing smile, as if she had seen this play out before. Life had a way of moving forward, whether you wanted it to or not, and she had learned long ago to flow with it, rather than fight against the current. The memory of last night, like so many others, *would find its place in the recesses of her mind—filed away under 'what could have been' but never truly was.*

Life moved on, and so did she. AV slowly faded into the background, transforming into nothing more than a distant memory—a brief footnote in the ongoing narrative of her life.

By the time a few days had passed and she had wrapped up her work calls and navigated the usual power struggle with her dotted-line manager over her travel arrangements, AV was already drifting from her thoughts, like the details of a dream slipping away with each passing day. The demands of her daily life soon took precedence, and she moved on, his presence in her mind growing more transient, like the remnants of a tune you can't quite place.

There were projects to manage, emails to answer, and decisions to make. As the days turned into weeks, the intensity of that night with AV began to dissipate, replaced by the comforting rhythm of her daily routine. The demands of her work pulled her back into a familiar orbit, where deadlines and deliverables took precedence over lingering thoughts of what could have been.

What had seemed so significant in the moment now felt almost trivial in hindsight, as though time had worn down the edges of those memories, making them softer, less defined, easier to let go.

And so, she let it go—let him go—without much effort, like a leaf carried away by the wind, drifting further out of sight with each passing day. There was no room for distractions, no time for what-ifs.

Weeks drifted by, and AV barely crossed her mind—until one evening, a text from him blinked onto her screen like an unexpected guest. *The timing was curious, almost as if the universe had nudged him to reach out just when she had finally stopped wondering about him.*

His name, once a flutter in her chest, now appeared with the same casualness as a message from a distant acquaintance. He was in her city and wanted to meet. The words were simple, unassuming, but they carried the weight of unanswered questions and unresolved feelings.

RoKo stared at the message, a cocktail of surprise and mild irritation stirring within her. *Why now?* she thought, her mind replaying the last time they had spoken—the polite brush-off, the absence of any follow-up, the silence that had stretched on like an unfinished sentence.

His earlier brush-off had left a sour taste, one that she wasn't keen on revisiting. It was like reopening a book you had deliberately set aside, knowing the plot wouldn't change, no matter how many times you read it.

Her fingers hovered over the keyboard, the temptation to ignore him entirely hanging in the air. She could almost see herself tossing her phone onto the bed, letting the message go unanswered, a silent statement of her indifference.

But with a slight smirk, she tapped out a reply, her sarcasm veiled in politeness: "Sorry, I can't. I've got a BROKEN LEG, so I'm out of commission for a while."

The lie rolled off her fingers effortlessly, a small act of rebellion against the predictability of his sudden reappearance. She hit send, the lie as smooth as the wine they had once shared. A part of her wondered if he would catch the tone, the subtle hint that this was no coincidence but a choice—to keep him at arm's length, to not give in to the allure of what could have been, something that had once started at Alloro.

His response was swift, almost mechanical: "Get well soon." There was no follow-up question, no concern about the absurdity of her excuse—*just a clean, impersonal reply that felt like the end of a transaction.*

RoKo stared at the screen for a moment longer, her smirk gradually softening into a knowing smile. It was clear now—whatever fleeting connection they had shared had drifted out to the sea, carried away by the tides of time and disinterest.

And with that, she placed her phone down, the text already becoming another small, insignificant moment in the broader scheme of things in her life. The evening continued, uninterrupted, and so did she, moving forward with the same grace and resolve that had always been her way.

But as Armaan sent the text, a pang of sadness settled in. He hadn't expected to feel this way—missing the opportunity to see her again, wondering if she was truly hurt or just trying to avoid him. Should he go and visit her? The thought lingered for a moment, but then he shook his head, trying to dismiss it. "Oh no, come on, I hardly know her," he muttered to himself.

And then, as if on cue, Froggy sprang to life in his mind, *"She was your one-night stand, Armaan. Now stop bothering yourself. She's already avoiding you, and here you are, reeling in her thoughts! How stupid is that?"* The words echoed in his head, sharp and insistent, pulling him back to reality.

Armaan sighed, feeling a mix of frustration and disappointment. Froggy was right, wasn't he? It was just one night—just a fleeting moment in time. But then why did it feel like more? He brushed the thought aside, deciding it was time to let it go, to stop letting his mind wander back to RoKo. Yet, even as he tried to push her out of his thoughts, a part of him couldn't help but wonder—what if?

And just like that, the thread of their story unraveled before it even had the chance to be woven into something more.

The words on their screens faded into the background, much like the memory they had in their mind of each other. It was almost amusing, how the connection that once seemed so significant had fizzled out into a mere footnote. There was no drama, no grand declaration of feelings, just a casual dismissal—like an unfinished book they had lost interest in.

RoKo chuckled softly to herself imagining his reaction—if there was one at all. Perhaps he was relieved, dodging an awkward reunion that could have shattered whatever illusion they had both built up that night. Or perhaps, just perhaps, there was a whisper of regret on his side too, a passing thought that something could have developed. But the truth?

She didn't care enough to dwell on it. The city outside her window buzzed with life, full of possibilities, full of stories waiting to be lived—and she had no intention of lingering in a past that barely existed.

The story didn't need an ending because it never truly began

Two strangers met in a city far from home, shared a few too many drinks, and engaged in a conversation that blurred into the haze of the night.

The details were fuzzy, lost in the fog of wine and laughter, except for one absurdly memorable moment—when Armaan, with a grin that could melt ice, claimed he had lost seven kilograms and decided to prove it by doing an impromptu catwalk across the room. *RoKo had insisted on a full view, not just a seated one, wanting to see exactly where those kilograms had vanished. And as he strutted with playful confidence, she couldn't help but feel her heart skip a beat.*

He was handsome in a way that almost seemed unfair—chiseled features, a boyish charm that lingered just beneath the surface, and a presence that filled the room effortlessly. He was everything she had ever imagined her best self could be—charming, confident, and undeniably magnetic. It was as if she were staring at a male reflection of her own aspirations, the qualities she admired and longed to embody.

But as with all momentary illusions, reality has a way of creeping back in, much like dawn slowly chasing away the night.

What had seemed like a brief brush with something extraordinary—was, in truth, just another moment in the vastness of her life. AV, for all his allure, was simply a passing figure in her journey—*a spark that flared brightly but wasn't meant to last.*

As she tried to let the memory slip away, her familiar butterflies fluttered back, their tiny wings buzzing with judgment. They whispered how foolish she had been, how she had let herself get caught up in the fantasy of it all. *"You're such an idiot,"* they chided, their voices a chorus of regret and self-reproach. RoKo could almost hear their tiny voices mocking her, reminding her of the countless times she had let her guard down, only to be disappointed.

But this time, instead of arguing back or drowning in their reproach, she simply smiled—a small, familiar smile, a quiet reminder that the world doesn't pause for fleeting connections. And so, she too moved on, understanding that not every encounter is destined to become a story. Sometimes, people cross paths for a moment, sharing a brief chapter, only to continue on their separate journeys, each carrying a piece of the other but destined to go their separate ways.

FIVE

ARE THEY TO MEET AGAIN! OR ARE THEY DONE AND DUSTED!!!

While RoKo denied AV the pleasure of her company when he was in her city, a peristent feeling bugged her. It was subtle at first, like the faint hum of a distant echo, but as time wore on, it grew harder to ignore. Something didn't sit right, a tiny thread of unease that tugged at the edges of her thoughts, but she pushed it aside, convincing herself that it didn't matter. Yet, the feeling hung on, like a shadow that refused to disappear, no matter how brightly the lights around her shone.

AV seemed different—maybe out of her league, or maybe just too good to be true. There was a mystique about him, something that both intrigued and excited her, a combination that made him feel just a bit too unattainable.

Not that RoKo wasn't extraordinary in her own right. She effortlessly embodied a rare trifecta of smartness, charisma, and intellectual ability, making her stand out in any crowd. Her magnetic presence drew people in with a quiet confidence that spoke louder than words. Her energy was infectious, and she carried herself with an unmatched air of class. It wasn't just about her appearance, though she certainly turned heads without even trying.

RoKo had a natural elegance about her, a kind of grace that couldn't be taught or bought. She didn't need to put in much effort to look good—her taste was impeccable, gravitating toward things that were timeless, graceful, and undeniably classy.

She believed in having finer things in life, each piece carefully chosen to reflect her refined sense of style.

RoKo knew who she was and what she wanted, and that clarity gave her an edge that few others possessed. Yet, even with all her strengths, there hovered a doubt on this one in specific—the nagging question of whether someone like AV could see her for all she was, or if he had already dismissed her as just another fleeting encounter.

As the night deepened around her, RoKo found herself caught between two worlds: one where she embodied poise and sophistication, and the other where insecurities lurked in the shadows, whispering that maybe, just maybe, she wasn't quite enough.

But just as quickly as the thought surfaced, she pushed it away, letting her trademark confidence take over once more. After all, RoKo wasn't the kind of woman who dwelt in self-doubt. She was a woman who knew her worth and wasn't afraid to own it.

Was it because, deep down, she wondered if there could have been something more? Or was it simply the residual impact of their brief but intense connection? The kind of connection that lingers long after the moment has passed, leaving a faint, almost imperceptible trace on the heart.

Whatever it was, RoKo didn't dwell on it for too long. She was too grounded, too self-assured to let it bother her.

She had faced far greater challenges before and had emerged stronger every time. This, too, would pass, leaving her even more resilient. So, with a confident smile, RoKo pushed AV and the what-ifs from her mind, focusing instead on the present moment. There was work to be done, people to meet, and goals to achieve.

She carried herself with the assurance that she was exactly where she needed to be, doing exactly what she needed to do.

And then, just like that, a few days turned into weeks, and weeks turned into months. Armaan became out of sight and out of mind, fading into the background of RoKo's bustling life.

But one day, as she casually flipped through a magazine, she stumbled upon a full-page ad featuring Armaan's interview. It was a glossy, polished spread, the kind that catches eye with its sharp visuals and bold headlines.

In an instant, his image came alive in her mind, stirring up memories she thought had been buried. The way he had laughed, the way his eyes had sparkled with mischief—it all rushed back to her with an unsettling intensity.

Without a second thought, RoKo decided to text him. The message was simple, just a casual attempt to reconnect, to bridge the gap that time had created. But when AV didn't respond, she felt a wave of frustration. It wasn't just about the lack of a reply—it was about what that silence represented.

To her, it felt discourteous, dismissive even, feeding into the gnawing doubt that maybe she hadn't meant as much to him as she thought.

Her mind began to churn, feeding the devil within her thoughts. *Who does he think he is?* she thought bitterly. *He doesn't even have the decency to respond. Sure, everyone is busy, so am I.*

Yet, I always find time to reply to messages because what you make important becomes important.

Her thoughts spiraled, turning over each possibility, each reason why he might have chosen not to reply.

Was it deliberate? Had he simply moved on, casting her aside like an afterthought? Or was it something else, something deeper that she couldn't quite put her finger on?

The silence was maddening, not just because it left her hanging, but because it opened up a Pandora's box of insecurities she thought she had long buried.

As the day wore on, the frustration clung like a stubborn stain, refusing to be washed away. But beneath the frustration, there was something else—a simmering curiosity, a desire to understand why his silence bothered her so much.

She knew she shouldn't care, shouldn't let it get under her skin. Yet, here she was, replaying their brief encounters, searching for clues, trying to piece together a puzzle that had no clear solution

The more she dwelled on it, the more her frustration grew, morphing into a kind of righteous indignation. She found herself pacing, her mind replaying snippets of their past interactions, now tinged with the bitterness of disappointment.

Why had she even bothered? Was it just to satisfy her curiosity? Or was there something deeper, something she hadn't been willing to admit to herself?

As the hours passed with still no word from AV, RoKo finally let out a sigh of resignation. Maybe this was for the best. Maybe the universe that had brought them together, that same very universe was now telling her to leave the past where it belonged—in the past. But even as she tried to push the thoughts away, the nagging feeling of being dismissed weighed on her, making it hard to find peace.

She sat down, staring at her phone, willing herself to let it go, to move on. Yet, a part of her couldn't help but feel a sting—a sting that perhaps she had been too quick to trust, too quick to believe that what they shared had been anything more than a fleeting moment.

Maybe AV's silence wasn't about her at all. Maybe it was about him, about whatever shadows he kept hidden, the ones he wasn't ready to share with anyone, not even someone who had momentarily glimpsed beyond his polished surface.

With a deep breath, RoKo decided to let it be, to let the unanswered message hang in the air like a mystery left unsolved. After all, not every story needs a neat ending. Some are meant to remain open, with just enough room for possibilities, no matter how unlikely they might seem. Life, as always, would move on, and so would she—knowing that, for now, this chapter was better left unfinished.

However, she could not stop from keeping her monologue on—*maybe he just doesn't respect people. Maybe I was just another fleeting moment in his busy life, nothing more than a blip on his radar.*

The thoughts kept looping, like a mental tug-of-war that refused to let go, pulling her deeper into a sea of self-doubt. *But I shouldn't care this much,* she reminded herself, *AV isn't worth this much of your energy.*

She tried to convince herself that he was just another charming guy, likely surrounded by a sea of admirers who were eager to give him all the attention he craved. *Why should I be any different?* she mused, feeling like just one more insignificant addition to his crowd of cheerleaders.

Determined to shake off these thoughts, RoKo dove headfirst into her work, hoping to lose herself in the steady rhythm of emails and late night meetings.

Yet, no matter how focused she tried to be, AV's name kept flashing through her mind like a persistent pop-up ad that wouldn't close. *Why didn't he respond?* she fumed silently, her irritation growing with each passing hour. *This is so rude.*

The mental seesaw game continued for what felt like an eternity, her mind flipping back and forth between the tasks at hand and the enigma that was AV.

And then, her phone started buzzing. She glanced at the screen, her heart skipping a beat when she saw his name glowing there like an unexpected guest. Her pulse quickened, her breath catching in her throat. *Is this real? It felt almost surreal, like one of those cartoon moments where stars fill the protagonist's eyes, dazzling and disorienting. She couldn't remember the last time someone had this effect on her, this dizzying mix of excitement and anxiety.*

Why him? she wondered, trying to make sense of the emotions that were swirling inside her like a storm. *What is it about him that stirs these feelings within me?*

It was as if her body was reacting independently, a surge of dopamine rushing through her veins, leaving her feeling both exhilarated and unsteady. *AV was like a sudden hit of dopamine, an electrifying rush that she couldn't quite explain but couldn't ignore either.*

RoKo took a deep breath, forcing herself to steady the wild flutter of her heart. *Get a grip,* she silently commanded herself, striving for composure. With as much coolness as she could muster, she answered the phone, her voice deliberately low and sophisticated. "Hello," she said, keeping her tone calm, even as her insides churned with a mix of anticipation and curiosity.

"Hey," AV replied, his voice casual and smooth, almost too casual. *Isn't he the charmer?* RoKo thought, suppressing an eye roll. "You don't have to be so formal. You don't need to text me; you can just call."

RoKo bit back the sarcastic retort that bubbled up in her throat. *Oh, really? As if you actually attend to calls and texts.* But she swallowed the words, letting them die unspoken.

AV's casual approach only added fuel to the confusing mix of emotions she was grappling with. This wasn't just about AV anymore—it was about what he symbolized for her. *Why am I getting so attached to him?* she wondered, or rather, *to the idea of him.*

It dawned on her that her attachment wasn't just to AV as a person; it was to the image she had constructed in her mind.

The idea of AV was intoxicating, almost addictive, but she knew it was also dangerous, blurring the delicate lines between reality and fantasy.

This might just be infatuation, she thought, but for now, she chose to indulge in the moment. She allowed herself to enjoy the thrill, the rush that came with hearing his voice on the other end of the line.

There would be time later to figure out what all of this truly meant, to separate the reality from the fantasy. For now, she was content to let the dopamine do its work, to savor the high of something that might be just a little too good to be true.

"How are you doing? How's the BROKEN LEG and how is the recovery going? Are you okay now?" AV's voice had an edge of genuine concern that caught RoKo slightly off guard. *She had completely forgotten about the broken leg story she gave Armaan the last time.* RoKo quickly composed herself, slipping back into the role she had created. "Yeah, I'm fine," she replied, trying to sound casual. "I just got the plaster off. I'm on physio now, and I've started going back to work and my regular travels. What about you?"

"Well, work is keeping me very busy, as usual," Armaan responded, but there was a playful tone in his voice. "But I guess you're busier than me, huh?"

There was something in his words that made RoKo pause, a subtle hint that he might have expected more from her—perhaps a stronger connection after everything that had happened. *She should have known by now that it's difficult for me to make the first move,* Armaan mused internally, a twinge of frustration creeping in. But before he could dwell on it, Froggy, his ever-present inner voice, interrupted with a mocking tone. *"Seriously, Armaan? You think she's buying that? After all your knocking, joking, and locking? You're expecting her to believe you can't make the first move?"* Froggy's words hit home, and Armaan knew he was right.

That night, it had been AV who took the first step, who initiated everything. And now, here he was, waiting for RoKo to make the first move. It was a strange role reversal that didn't quite sit well with him, but he brushed it off, refocusing on the conversation.

RoKo, sensing the slight awkwardness, smiled to herself. "Maybe, yeah. Both of us are busy." She hesitated for a moment before adding, "I'm headed to Bangalore next week for four days. I've got a conference to attend."

"Wow," exclaimed Armaan, suddenly more animated. "I'm going to be there too! What are your dates?" he asked, his curiosity piqued. When they realized they had a two-day overlap, his excitement was palpable. "Hey, tell me where you're booked. Let me see if I can check in there as well."

As RoKo and AV talked further, RoKo couldn't shake the feeling that this connection was more than just a simple crush. It felt like a reflection, a mirror held up to her own soul, showing her both her strengths and her vulnerabilities

HUH! We're doing this again? RoKo thought to herself, a mixture of surprise and amusement flickering in her eyes, wasn't the coldness of the next morning not enough to stop this going from anywhere afar.

In Armaan's mind, he could barely contain his excitement. *Wow, we're doing it again!* he thought, feeling a sense of serendipity wash over him.

This wasn't about anything physical—far from it. In fact, nothing remotely physical had happened between them. They hadn't even properly shaken hands, aside from that one brief, almost accidental Hi Five.

But there was something else, something that lingered in the space between them, something intangible yet undeniably powerful. It was like a current, an undercurrent that neither of them could quite place but both could feel.

Whenever they were near each other, it was as if the very air around them shifted, charged with an energy that was both thrilling and unsettling.

An unspoken tension hung between them, not the kind that demanded resolution, but the kind that thrived in its own ambiguity, adding layers of complexity to every glance, every word exchanged.

It was as if the universe had decided to play a game with them, weaving an invisible thread that kept pulling them together, even when logic suggested they should remain apart. Each encounter of theirs felt like a step closer to some unknown destination, a place neither of them could see but both were inexplicably drawn toward.

They both knew there was something more beneath the surface, but neither dared to disturb it, afraid that naming it would somehow break the spell.

So, they let it be, let it grow in the quiet spaces between their words, each of them wondering, waiting, what would happen if they ever let this invisible connection fully take shape.

It was the kind of connection that left them both curious, intrigued, and just a little bit terrified—because deep down, they both knew that once that line was crossed, there would be no going back.

SIX

FAST FORWARD 11 MONTHS AND 11 DAYS — THE HEARTBREAK...

It was almost as if their entire relationship had been following an invisible script, one they hadn't even realized they were acting out. And now, just like everything had fallen into place when they met, things were quietly unraveling. In all the time they'd known each other, Armaan had never once taken back the key card to RoKo's suite. No matter how much she asked, he always found reasons to refuse, reasons he never fully explained. But this one time—just this once—he did.

And what he walked into felt like it had been waiting for him all along. Chaos. Disarray. It was almost as if fate had decided to step in and pull them apart, the same way it had brought them together. It felt eerie, like the universe was telling them that their story had reached its end. Maybe, in some way, they both knew it. They had played their parts, and now, there was nothing left to say, nothing left to do. Just the quiet acceptance that this chapter was closing.

With long, determined steps, clutching the key to her luxurious suite, Armaan moved like a man on a mission. He had promised RoKo a quick visit before picking up his boss and heading off on his business trip. His thoughts were set on sharing one last breakfast together. Dressed casually yet with a touch of understated elegance—his snug olive green T-shirt accentuating his athletic build and well-worn jeans hinting at countless comfortable travels—Armaan, with his MacBook clutched under one arm, was calm, unaware of the storm ahead.

But the moment he entered the room, his steps faltered. Something was wrong. The peaceful morning light bathed the room, but instead of tranquility, chaos greeted him. A vase, tipped over, trickled water across the floor, scattered clothes lay like abandoned thoughts, and empty bottles and glasses littered the table. The elegant decor now felt jarringly out of place amidst the mess. A cold sense of disbelief washed over him—this wasn't what he had expected.

His breath tightened as his eyes darted from one sign of disarray to the next. His grip on the MacBook grew tighter, anger slowly building under his skin, bubbling into something uncontrollable. What was meant to be a calm visit quickly became the spark for his rising storm.

He stood at the foot of the bed, towering over her as she slept. His presence was a jarring intrusion into her peaceful morning. With a booming "hello," Armaan jolted RoKo awake. Her eyelids fluttered open, her mind still foggy, but his blazing eyes snapped her into reality.

As he scanned the room once again—clothes haphazardly piled on the floor, plates and cutlery in disarray, and those damn empty bottles—his initial shock quickly morphed into something darker. His pulse quickened, his grip around the MacBook tightening even further as the fury surged within him.

"What the hell happened here?" he demanded, his voice slicing through the silence, each word sharp with disbelief. His jaw clenched in frustration. RoKo blinked, startled by the sudden intensity, her heart racing as she sat up in bed. The air between them thickened, his accusation hanging in the room like the mess that surrounded them.

He had asked her—no, he had commanded her—to put the phone away and just sleep. He had tucked her into bed just a few hours earlier, kissed her goodnight, and watched as she almost drifted off, her eyes drowsy—whether from sleep or the alcohol, he couldn't tell. But now, he was seething with rage, convinced that her actions were a betrayal. As RoKo looked at him, still groggy from the previous night's hangover, he shouted, "Why did you pick up your damn phone?" his voice rising. He had taken the phone from her, switched it off, and placed it far away. He had done it for her, for he cared for her, to protect her from herself. Or so he claimed. But was it really care, or just another way to exert control?

In Armaan's mind, the outburst felt like a scene torn from his troubled past. Anger hit him like a crashing wave, driven by an unsettling sense of déjà vu. It was as if he was trapped in a painful replay, watching a hauntingly familiar movie unfold. The echoes of old betrayals roared through him, merging with the fresh pain and leaving him overwhelmed. The boundaries between past and present dissolved, throwing him into a tumultuous storm of raw, chaotic emotions.

He stormed out of the room, his final words hanging in the air like a death knell: "We are done." For a moment, time seemed to freeze around RoKo. She stood there, her heart pounding, trying to process the weight of those three words. Still reeling from the hangover, her thoughts raced, colliding with the reality that was quickly crumbling around her. It was as if the world had spun off its axis, leaving her disoriented and numb. She called out after him, her voice breaking with desperation, pleading for him to return. Her tone quivered, filled with an urgency that seemed to echo through the walls. Later, when he finally answered the phone, his voice was chillingly distant. "I'm never coming back," he said, each word sharp and unyielding. The finality of his statement struck her like a physical blow, leaving her breathless and stunned. He repeated his questions cutting through the silence with relentless intensity: "Why did you pick up your damn phone? Why did you call those people?"

Armaan was someone who couldn't bring himself to say the words "I love you". It wasn't that he didn't feel something for her; in fact, his feelings for her were intense, complicated, and often overwhelming. But love, for Armaan, was a word loaded with expectations, vulnerability, and a loss of control that terrified him. To say "I love you" meant opening up a part of himself that he had kept locked away for years—a part of him that had been hurt deeply before.

He had learned from past relationships that love could be a double-edged sword. In his mind, love was dangerous because it meant letting someone in, giving them the power to hurt you. Armaan had been hurt before, blindsided by someone he had once loved deeply, and the wounds from that experience had never truly healed. The scars remained, a constant reminder of the pain he had vowed never to experience again.

So when it came to RoKo, he kept those three words at bay, choosing instead to say "I care for you." It was safer, less binding. "Caring" implied concern and affection without the depth and vulnerability that "love" demanded. It allowed him to maintain control, to keep a part of himself guarded and protected.

Armaan believed that if he didn't say "I love you," then he wouldn't have to deal with the mess that could follow—expectations, responsibilities, the fear of not being enough, or worse, being hurt again.

In his mind, caring for RoKo was enough. It was his way of showing that he was there for her and invested in their relationship, without crossing an invisible line into territory that felt too perilous. He convinced himself that "I care for you" would suffice, believing RoKo would understand this as his way of expressing his feelings and commitment. However, to RoKo, the words "care for you" rang hollow. In all their 11 months and 11 days together, he had never once said he loved her. It was always "I care for you," as if that alone sufficed. To her, it wasn't just a question of care—it felt like a form of control.

And deep down, Armaan also knew that this wasn't enough. He knew that RoKo deserved more than half-measures, more than a guarded heart that refused to fully open up to her. Yet, he couldn't bring himself to say it.

Every time RoKo looked at him with those eyes that seemed to ask for more, for that one word he couldn't say, Armaan felt a pang of guilt. He could see the hurt in her eyes, the confusion as to why he could never bring himself to say what she needed to hear. He could sense the growing distance between them, a chasm that widened every time he chose to say "I care for you".

Armaan wasn't blind to the fact that his inability to express love was driving a wedge between them. But admitting that, confronting the reasons why he couldn't say those words, would mean facing the very demons he had spent years avoiding. It would mean acknowledging the fear that still held him captive, the fear that even with RoKo, who was everything he could want, he might still lose himself in the process. And so, even as he watched RoKo slowly slip away, he did nothing to stop it.

Even in the blur of her hungover haze, RoKo knew why she had really picked up the phone. It wasn't just a call—it was the last tether to something she couldn't admit she was losing.

Her world had crumbled, slowly, painfully, until the weight of it felt unbearable. She wasn't herself, not in mind or heart. Yesterday had been a promise—one that slipped away before she could hold onto it. She and AV were supposed to return from Bangalore to Chennai together, a road trip just for the two of them. A long, uninterrupted drive with him behind the wheel, the kind of trip that filled her with excitement and something more—hope.

But lately, AV had been distant. His smile never quite reached his eyes anymore, his warmth felt like it was slipping through her fingers, no matter how tightly she tried to hold on. In the morning, when he left the hotel, he had said he would pick her up by 2 p.m., or tell her where to meet near the highway and they would drive down to Chennai once he was done with his meetings. It was going to be their time. Finally.

RoKo had woken up early, excited like she hadn't been in a long time. She packed her bags with care, savoring the idea of the trip ahead. A lazy breakfast followed, each bite filled with anticipation. But by noon, something shifted.

No message. No call.

By 1 p.m., her stomach churned with unease, not hunger. The minutes stretched longer than they should have. And still, nothing.

It was 2 p.m. and AV was nowhere. Eleven months they had spent together, and yet she still hadn't figured out why he pulled away like this—why he became someone she could hardly recognize at times.

By 3 p.m., the silence had become unbearable. She had waited long enough. Then, at 3:15 p.m., her phone buzzed. The message read: "Sorry, some impromptu change of plans. We'll have to drive separately. I've got people I can't say no to. We'll catch up in Chennai. I'll meet you at the hotel later tonight."

Thankfully her driver was on standby, a contingency she never thought she'd need, not today. The bags that she had so joyfully packed were loaded into the car, along with the snacks she'd planned for the road trip. But this wasn't how it was supposed to go. Not in some rented SUV, alone.

It should have been her and AV, the road stretching out before them, endless conversations filling the car, laughter breaking through the hum of the engine. Now, the drive felt cold. The luxury of the car meant nothing in the hollow space of her chest.

About 45 minutes in, she asked the driver to pull over at a shop. She wanted to feel numb, just for a while. "Four cans of beer and four bottles of soda," she had said, her voice mechanical, hollow.

But as the driver reached the shop and turned off the engine, something tugged at her. "Just soda," she corrected, the words leaving her before she could reconsider. Even in her emotional fog, there was a part of her that resisted the easy escape. A fragment of clarity, fighting to stay afloat.

And so, in the quiet of the long drive, with only the hum of the engine and the occasional jolt of the road beneath her, RoKo did what she often did—she let herself think. Really think. She returned calls she had been meaning to make, spoke to friends and family, filling the silence with familiar voices. But one of those calls changed everything.

In the middle of what seemed like an ordinary conversation with an acquaintance unaware of her connection to AV, a shocking truth surfaced—AV had two kids. Two kids, wow, seriously, he had never once mentioned to her. A truth he had hidden so deeply, it felt like it shattered whatever fragile connection remained between them.

She remembered a time when she stumbled upon a photograph of a child with Armaan that didn't sit right with her, leaving a nagging question she couldn't quite bring herself to ask. When she finally confronted him, his only response was, "You know the answer," dismissing it as if it meant nothing

But she hadn't known the full truth. Not really. Not like this. He had kept this part of his life sealed away, hidden from her, and now she understood just how much he had been holding back.

It was devastating. A betrayal she hadn't seen coming. The weight of it settled over her like a cold, suffocating blanket. She couldn't wrap her mind around it. How could he have kept something so important from her? What was he protecting? Himself? Her? It didn't matter. It only made the distance between them feel sharper, more painful.

They had been clear from the beginning—they weren't exclusive, and there was no future between them. That much had been spelled out. But even so, why hadn't he told her this? Why let her discover it this way? The questions swirled in her mind, unanswered, cutting deeper with each passing moment.

Tears welled up in her eyes, and soon, they fell silently down her cheeks. She was broken, her heart aching in ways she hadn't anticipated. But even in her hurt, she wasn't ready to confront him. Not yet. Not over the phone. Maybe later in the evening, when she could face him with all the weight of what she had just learned. For now, she would carry the burden alone, unsure of where they stood, or if they stood at all.

When RoKo arrived at the hotel, she barely noticed her surroundings. The weight of everything had settled too heavily on her chest. Without a second thought, she checked in and headed straight for the lounge. She needed to numb herself—anything to dull the sharp ache that had been gnawing at her since the drive.

By the time AV showed up, he was in a rush. He barely paused to take a breath before explaining that he needed to leave, promising they'd meet tomorrow for breakfast. It felt like a rehearsed line, practiced and distant. RoKo listened, her heart heavy with the hurricane of emotions that swirled inside her. She knew there was a critical project AV was working on, one that could skyrocket his career, and as much as she wanted to scream, to demand answers, she swallowed her pain. This wasn't the right moment, not for him. He didn't love her, that much had become painfully clear. But she loved him.

And because she loved him, she chose to care. In ways he never could.

AV offered to stay for a quick drink, but by then, RoKo was already two drinks in, her mind clouded and emotions raw. Each sip had done little to quiet the storm in her heart. After their rushed drink, he walked her back to her room, a fleeting gesture of care. He tucked her into bed, taking her phone away like she was a fragile thing that might break if left unattended. "Get some sleep," he said softly, as if that could solve anything.

But inside her, it wasn't just a storm—it was a hurricane, building and thrashing with every moment. She wasn't at peace. The betrayal she felt, the secrets he had kept, tore through her with a force she hadn't anticipated. And once AV left, the emptiness of the room closed in on her.

That's when she decided she couldn't hold it in anymore. She needed to vent, to release the chaos that churned inside her. RoKo picked up her phone and started dialing, ready to make all the calls she had been avoiding, unable to keep the weight of it all bottled up any longer.

Her dad had called earlier, just as she was with AV, and she had promised herself she would return his call once AV left.

RoKo always gave AV her full attention, focusing entirely on him whenever they were together, even when she felt like she was crumbling inside. But as soon as he was gone, and the room settled into an uneasy quiet, her mind refused to let her rest. Sleep became impossible—her thoughts racing back to the promise she had made to her father.

So, she picked up the phone. What started as a simple call to her dad quickly spiralled into something she hadn't planned for. Vulnerable and already drunk, she found herself dialing her mom next, then her sister, and then another friend. Each conversation pulled her deeper into her feelings, each voice giving her a momentary distraction from the hollow ache inside.

Before she realized it, she was on a video call with her best friend, a half-empty bottle of wine now in hand. The more she drank, the more the loneliness seemed to cling to her, despite the flood of familiar voices. And when even that wasn't enough, when the silence in her heart became unbearable, she reached for more—calling her ex, then another friend in the US, desperately seeking comfort wherever she could find it.

As the night dragged on, her phone buzzed with the constant flow of messages from others who cared—WhatsApp notifications from people who loved her, people who knew her strength and were drawn to her even more when they sensed her pain. Yet despite all the conversations, all the voices trying to fill the void, the loneliness still sat heavily in the room, unshaken.

RoKo was a storm in her own right—fierce, unpredictable, and impossible to contain. When she was distressed, it was as if the air around her charged with electricity, and everyone felt the pull to be near her, to offer whatever comfort they could. But Armaan had never truly grasped this part of her, had he? He always stood outside the eye of the storm, untouched by the winds that tore through her.

As the last call ended, her emotions still raged, swirling like a tempest inside her—unresolved, raw, and untamed. The entire bottle of wine was gone, four Hoegaarden pints downed in quick succession, yet the alcohol barely touched the ache that clawed at her chest. The room spun, but her pain remained sharp. Drunk, hurting, and desperate for release, she broke. The sobs came first—deep, guttural, each one tearing at her throat—followed by a flood of tears. She shouted into the empty room, her voice cracking until the words became nothing but hoarse, unintelligible cries.

In a daze, she stumbled into the bathroom, her legs weak and her mascara streaking down her cheeks like dark rivers. The mirror reflected a face she barely recognized—her eyes red-rimmed and wild, her mouth twisted in anguish. She didn't care. The need to escape her own skin overwhelmed her. She stepped into the bathtub filled and ready for a soak, clothes and all, the cold porcelain pressing against her as she sank into it, curling her knees up to her chest.

The water soaked her clothes, plastering them to her skin, seeping into her hair, her flesh, and deeper—into her soul. She sobbed until the tears ran dry, her face sticky with the remnants of mascara and salt, her breaths coming in shaky gasps. The bathroom lights buzzed above, harsh and unforgiving, casting sharp shadows that seemed to close in on her.

At some point, time blurred. She dragged herself out of the tub, water pooling at her feet, soaking the tile floor. Her wet clothes clung to her like a second skin, heavy and cold, leaving a trail of droplets behind her as she stumbled toward the bed. She barely made it to the edge before collapsing, curling into a ball beneath the sheets, still drenched.

Flashback:

She and AV were supposed to spend two days together in Bangalore, followed by a day in Chennai. Their trips had become a ritual—days spent wrapped in each other's company, as if the outside world didn't exist. But this time felt different. Heavier. The air between them had thickened with unspoken tensions. AV knew RoKo was struggling, drowning in a phase of her life where even getting out of bed felt like a triumph. She had told him, in broken pieces, about the antidepressants and sleeping pills she relied on just to make it through each day. But the pills only muted the world around her, dulling the sharp edges without ever truly lifting the darkness.

And now, wine had become her latest refuge—a liquid escape that numbed her faster than the pills ever could. In AV's presence, she would pour glass after glass, losing count as the pain slowly ebbed into a dull throb. With him, she felt some small measure of safety, though it was fleeting, fragile. She would cry openly, her emotions spilling over with each sip—uncontrolled, raw, like a dam that had finally cracked.

AV had watched her with an uneasy detachment, as though her suffering was an inconvenience. To him, her tears seemed over the top, exaggerated—like she was making too much of nothing. He tolerated it, but he didn't truly see her. He didn't stop her either, letting her spiral, perhaps out of habit. He had grown accustomed to her presence, to the chaos she carried with her—so much so that he now spent more time with her than some of his oldest friends.

There was one night, after too many glasses of wine, that the words RoKo had kept buried for so long finally broke free. She looked at him, her eyes heavy with vulnerability, and asked the question that had been clawing at her for months. "Hey, how close are we, AV? Are we... mutually exclusive?" Her voice trembled, carrying a raw mix of hope and fear, as though she was grasping for something solid to hold onto—anything to make sense of the almost-year they had spent together.

But AV didn't answer. The silence stretched between them, thick and unbearable, like a storm cloud hanging in the air that refused to break. RoKo's heart pounded against her ribs as she repeated herself, her desperation more palpable this time. Finally, he responded, but his answer was a single, cold word: "No."

The word sliced through her, sharp and merciless. It left her reeling, yet again, from an emotional wound she hadn't expected. She had given nearly a year of her life to this man, sharing pieces of herself that she hadn't shown anyone else, yet she knew almost nothing about him. AV was always guarded, a locked vault she had no key for, while he expected her to remain wide open, exposed.

She wanted to dig deeper, to pry open his silence and make sense of it, to understand what they truly were to each other. But each time she tried, AV would sidestep her questions with ease. He was a master at deflecting, turning her painful inquiries into a joke or a story, sometimes pouring her another glass of wine as if the alcohol could wash away her doubts. It became clear that AV wasn't just avoiding the question—he was avoiding the truth. Whatever existed between them, he was too afraid to name it, too afraid to confront it.

And so, they continued their uneven dance. RoKo laid her heart bare, piece by piece, while AV kept his hidden behind walls, offering her just enough to keep her near but never enough to truly let her in.

RoKo knew she was caught in a cycle—one she longed to escape but couldn't quite bring herself to leave. It was like she was bound to AV by invisible threads.

The next thing she knew, AV was standing over her, his eyes sharp, a storm of accusation brewing in his gaze. "What happened here?" His voice cut through the room, cold and full of suspicion, as if the mess around them was some kind of betrayal. RoKo blinked, her mind foggy, but the evidence of her unraveling was everywhere—a shattered wine glass glinting on the floor, chips crushed into the carpet, the empty wine bottle lying on its side, the four Hoegaarden pints drained and scattered, and her soaked clothes discarded in a pile as Armaan looked closely at the chaos.

It all mirrored the emotional wreckage inside her, laid bare for him to see.

AV's voice tightened, his demand for answers slicing through the air. He didn't understand, couldn't grasp the depth of her turmoil, but still, he needed control. "Give me your phone," he snapped, as though the device held the key to whatever he imagined had happened. RoKo, too drained to fight, too empty to resist, simply handed it over, her body moving before her mind could catch up. In that moment, she wasn't just handing over her phone—she was surrendering.

He scrolled through her phone—through the calls, the messages, the names—each flick of his finger igniting his anger. "Why did you call these people? Why did you call all these men?" His voice was thick with accusation, the words dripping with jealousy and suspicion. It didn't matter to him that she had called everyone, not just men. He was blind to reason, or maybe he simply didn't care. He was projecting, letting his own fears twist into something ugly, seeing betrayal where there was none.

AV's fury grew as though he had walked in on her with another man, his jealousy rising in waves, suffocating the room. Every word was laced with venom, each sentence an attack. RoKo, still dazed, her mind struggling to break through the alcohol's lingering fog, couldn't fully grasp what was happening. She reached out, her hand trembling as she tried to place it gently on his arm—a small gesture, a desperate attempt to calm the storm between them.

But he recoiled, pulling away from her touch as though it burned.

"I can explain," she started, her voice weak, pleading, but AV didn't care for explanations. His mind was already made up. He had decided who she was, and nothing she said could change that now.

"This is who you are," he spat, the words cutting through the air like a knife. "And we are done."

The force of those words hit RoKo like a blow to the gut. She felt them sink into her stomach, heavy and cold, reverberating through every inch of her body. What the hell did he mean by that? How could he judge her so harshly, reduce her to a single moment of weakness? Her vision blurred as tears began to spill, uncontrollable now, the dam of her restraint finally breaking.

How could he take everything they had shared—nearly a year of her life, her vulnerability, her trust—and reduce it to this? This wasn't about the wine, not really. It was about the pattern she had fallen into, one she thought she could escape but found herself trapped in again. It was about the shame she had carried for years.

"This is who you are." Those words echoed in her mind, dragging her back to her childhood, to her father's voice. She had heard them before, in a tone just as cold, just as dismissive. It was a phrase that had been used to punish her, to make her feel small, powerless, and unworthy. And now, standing before AV, it was as if she was reliving that trauma all over again—her heart splitting open in the same way it had back then.

The past was colliding with the present, and she didn't know how to survive it.

In that moment, RoKo couldn't connect the dots. Her mind was too clouded, too overwhelmed by AV's accusations to make sense of it all. She couldn't see how the pieces of her past were repeating themselves, playing out right in front of her. But the feeling—that deep, aching familiarity—was there. She just didn't understand it yet.

Growing up, she had been forbidden to even say hello to men or boys. A simple handshake? Unthinkable. If she dared to shake hands with someone, even if that was out of respect and courtesy, there would be consequences. Her father would make sure of that. To him, a handshake wasn't just an innocent gesture—it was a slippery slope, an invitation, a signal that she was too available, too easy. A handshake could mean the first step to the start of an affair, even if there was no basis in reality. The rules were rigid, suffocating, leaving her trapped under the weight of judgment she couldn't escape.

And now, here was AV, standing in front of her, making his own accusations. For him, chatting with men, being on a video call—this was a betrayal. In his mind, it meant something more, something darker. It wasn't just a conversation; it was promiscuity. As the words poured out of his mouth, RoKo couldn't help but feel like she had heard it all before. It was as if both AV and her father had been cut from the same cloth, woven together from the same thread of distrust and control.

Maybe that's why AV had always felt so familiar to her. The way he behaved, it mirrored her father's patterns so perfectly. Three days in a week, RoKo would mean a-lot to him. He'd give her his attention, his time, making her feel like she was his whole world. But then, like clockwork, he'd pull away for the rest four. Three days of closeness, and then the distance would settle in—like she didn't exist. Just like her father. The push and pull, the cycle of being loved and then erased—it was all too familiar.

But in that moment, she couldn't quite grasp it. She couldn't see how deeply this pattern had woven itself into her life, into her relationships. All she knew was the pain of being judged, being accused, being reduced to nothing more than the sum of someone else's fears and insecurities. It was the same hurt she had carried since childhood, and now it was staring her in the face once again.

And while the moment was painfully serious, there was something almost laughable about it all. Here was this man—who had declared they weren't mutually exclusive, who had hidden the fact that he had two kids for nearly a year—judging her, accusing her of betrayal. Seriously? Betrayal? This from the same AV who hadn't even bothered to share a detail as basic as having children, while RoKo knew the names, kids, and family details of even the security guard at work. The hypocrisy of it all would have been funny if it weren't so tragic.

As AV walked out of her life, slamming the door behind him, RoKo was left in a state of shock. The room felt suddenly empty, as if all the warmth and life had vanished the moment he walked out. Her legs gave way beneath her, and she collapsed onto the bed, burying her face in her hands as sobs wracked her body. His words played on a loop in her mind, stabbing at her heart each time she tried to make sense of them. How had it all gone so wrong? How could everything they had built together crumble so easily?

She thought about how much she had invested in this relationship—how much of herself she had poured into it. Every ounce of her love, trust, and vulnerability had been given freely, and yet he had walked away as if none of it mattered. *He didn't even give it a fight. That thought hit her harder than anything else. He didn't care enough to fight for them.*

But RoKo wasn't ready to give up. She had always been the one to piece things back together, to try again even when the cracks were too deep to heal. This time, it was no different. The fracture between them, this painful misunderstanding, couldn't be the end. She wiped away her tears, her breath still shaky as she tried to calm herself, to hold on to the remnants of what they had.

How could it all fall apart so easily? Over one misunderstanding? Over one night that spiraled out of control?

She remembered their laughter, their shared moments, now scattered like pieces of a broken mirror. Each fragment held a memory, a sliver of what they once were, and she believed—hoped—they could still put it back together. If only she could understand AV's side, maybe they could find their way back to each other. But deep down, a cold fear gnawed at her heart—the fear that AV had already begun to pull away, like a boat quietly drifting from the shore long before the storm even arrived.

Maybe, she thought sadly, he had been waiting for the perfect excuse to leave. And now, in this moment, he had found it—a reason to place the blame squarely on her shoulders. She could almost picture it, the guilt building inside him, wrapping tighter around his heart until it became unbearable. This was his escape, his way to shift the burden onto her, to make her the reason things had fallen apart. In his mind, it was easier to believe that it was RoKo's actions, her mistakes, that pushed them apart—not the slow fading of his own feelings. And with that, he could walk away, guilt-free, leaving her alone to pick up the shattered pieces of a relationship he had already let go.

Just yesterday, she had convinced herself that everything was fine, that their love was solid, just that AV was someone who needed time to express and open up. But now, the love she had fought so fiercely to protect was slipping away, and she felt powerless to stop it. But then it hit her—the bitter realization she had refused to see. It wasn't *their* love she was fighting for. It was *her* love. For AV, it was never love, only care. *"I care for you, RoKo."* That was all he ever said.

Her heart shattered as she came to terms with the harsh truth—AV had misunderstood her in the worst possible way. And that misunderstanding cut deeply, because it was rooted in his reality, not hers. His reality was one shaped by his own fears, insecurities, and emotional distance. It was a world so vastly different from hers that it created a chasm between them, one she could never hope to bridge.

AV couldn't see her vulnerability; he couldn't see her love.

He mistook her openness for weakness, and his dismissive attitude toward her feelings left her feeling utterly isolated, misunderstood in the worst way. The memories of that first night together resurfaced, uninvited and unwelcome, flooding her mind. She could still hear his voice, casually remarking how callous she must be to sit in a room full of half-drunk men. At the time, she had laughed it off, playing along as if it were harmless banter. But now, under the harsh light of his indifference, those words took on a darker, more sinister meaning.

"Has this been his perception of me all along?" RoKo wondered, her heart sinking with the realization. The very thought sent a shiver down her spine, leaving her feeling cheap and dirty, a stain she feared would cling to her forever.

In that moment, RoKo felt stripped of her dignity, her worth reduced to the careless judgment of a man who had never truly seen her. She felt exposed, raw, as if all her insecurities had been laid bare—not just to him, but to herself.

His words stung, but the wound went far deeper than she had anticipated. It wasn't just her heart that was wounded; it was her very sense of self. She felt tainted by his perception of her, reduced to a caricature of the woman she actually was—just another nameless figure in a room full of men, nothing more. The shame settled in her chest, a heavy, immovable weight she knew wouldn't lift easily.

This would leave a scar. A constant reminder of the danger of opening herself up to someone who was never willing to truly see her.

As she sat there, drowning in the overwhelming tide of emotions, RoKo made a silent vow to herself. Never again would she allow anyone to make her feel this way. Never again would she let her openness be mistaken for weakness. The rawness of the moment slowly began to shift into something else—resolve.

AV's trust issues, rooted in the scars of his past, had clouded his ability to see her for who she truly was.

But amidst the heartbreak, something within her shifted. The tears fell, but with each one, a deeper clarity emerged.She wiped them away, her hands trembling yet firm, and began to realize something profound: despite the pain AV had caused her, she had given him something he might not have realized—a little more compassion, a little more love, not just for her, but for himself and for the world.

As she sat there, a flood of memories hit RoKo, and one in particular flickered back to her mind—a night when AV had let his guard down, just once, and revealed a part of himself she rarely saw.

It had been one of those quiet nights, thick with unspoken tension, the kind that made everything feel more serious. The only light in the room came from a dim lamp, casting a warm, golden glow that softened the edges of their faces.

RoKo had been watching AV for a while, his usual confident demeanor replaced by something heavier, something that made him seem distant, like he was miles away. She leaned forward, a gentle smile on her lips. "You've been staring at that cushion for the last ten minutes," she teased lightly. "What's going on in that complicated head of yours?"

AV glanced up, met her eyes for the briefest moment, then looked away again. "It's nothing," he muttered, but the tension in his voice gave him away. "Just... thinking."

RoKo wasn't buying it. "Come on, you're a terrible liar," she said with a playful smirk, trying to coax him out of his shell. "I've seen you charm your way out of much worse. So, spill. What's on your mind?"

He sighed deeply, running a hand through his hair, clearly searching for the right words. "It's just..." he trailed off, hesitating. RoKo waited, her curiosity piqued, sensing something more than his usual evasions. Finally, he spoke, his voice low and raw. "Do you ever feel like... no matter what you do, it's never enough? Like you'll never be enough for the people who count on you?"

RoKo's heart ached hearing him admit that. This wasn't the AV who brushed off life like it couldn't touch him. This was someone burdened by fears he rarely let slip through the cracks.

"All the time," she said softly, leaning in. "But here's the thing—it's not about being enough for others. It's about being enough for yourself. And trust me, AV, you are. You just don't see it yet."

AV shook his head, a bitter laugh escaping him. "You make it sound so easy. But it's not. Every day, I wake up with this pressure... this fear that I'll let everyone down. That I'll fail and prove all those doubts right."

RoKo watched him closely, noticing how the words seemed to weigh him down. "Who's putting that pressure on you, AV? Is it really the people around you... or is it you? Are you the one setting impossible standards for yourself?"

There was a long silence. AV stared at the floor, thinking, before finally whispering, "Maybe it is me. Maybe I've always felt like if I'm not perfect, then it's not enough. And the thought of failing... it terrifies me."

RoKo reached out and took his hand, squeezing it gently. "AV, no one expects you to be perfect," she said, her voice full of warmth. "That's the myth. What matters is that you're trying. That's enough. And you're not alone in this—you've got people who care about you, who see how much you're worth, even when you don't."

AV stared down at their joined hands, his expression softening. "You really believe that?" he asked, a note of hope creeping into his voice.

"I do," RoKo replied, her grip on his hand tightening slightly. "And I'll believe it until you do too."

For the first time that night, AV looked at her—really looked at her—his eyes searching hers, as if trying to absorb the truth in her words. There was a vulnerability in his gaze, a side of him she rarely saw. "No one's ever believed in me like that," he said quietly, as if the words themselves were foreign to him.

RoKo smiled, the softness in her eyes undeniable. "Well, there's a first time for everything. And I'm not going anywhere."

AV's gaze softened further, and for a moment, the weight of the world seemed to lift just a little. "You're something else, you know that?" he said, a mix of admiration and gratitude in his voice.

"I've been told," RoKo replied, a playful glint in her eyes. "But don't think you're getting off the hook. We're tackling those fears of yours, one at a time."

AV chuckled, the sound lighter than it had been all night. "You make it sound like I've got a list of problems."

"We all do," RoKo said with a shrug. "But you're not facing them alone anymore. We're in this together."

In that moment, as they sat there with the night stretching ahead of them, AV realized that, for the first time in a long while, he didn't have to face his fears alone.

"So," RoKo said, breaking the comfortable silence that had wrapped around them, "how about we skip the deep talk and do something fun? Like, raid your fridge and see what kind of junk food you've got stashed away."

AV laughed, a real, hearty laugh that made RoKo's heart lighten. "You're on. But I'm warning you, my stash is pretty legendary."

"I'll be the judge of that," RoKo teased, standing up and pulling him along with her. "Come on, show me what you've got."

And just like that, the heavy atmosphere dissolved, replaced by a playful energy that brought easy smiles to their faces. As they rummaged through the fridge, tossing out half-empty cartons of takeout and bags of chips, their laughter filled the room, effortless and natural, like they had known each other forever. The connection between them deepened—not because of the heavy conversations, but because of moments like this. It was real, something that felt like it could last beyond just one night.

For that brief moment, the walls AV had built around his heart seemed to fall away, leaving him open, vulnerable. RoKo could see it—the fear, the hope, the yearning for something more. And as their eyes met across the kitchenette, she saw him as he truly was. Not the guarded man, but someone who wanted to be seen, someone who needed to be understood.

But even as she held his gaze, RoKo knew this moment was fragile. She knew those walls would come back up, maybe stronger than before. AV, with all his fears and insecurities, would retreat behind them again. But for now, she held onto the small victory of having seen him, even if just for a little while.

Off and on and still in the daze, RoKo reflected upon yet another particular moment, a night meant to be intimate and comforting. They had been seated across from each other at a cozy little restaurant, as she swirled the wine in her glass, she hesitated but finally gathered the courage to share the anxieties that had been weighing her down. "I've been feeling so overwhelmed lately," she said, her voice steady but fragile. "There's just so much pressure, and sometimes it feels like everything is closing in on me."

AV looked up from his plate, his face unreadable, his expression a wall she couldn't seem to break through. "You're overthinking again, RoKo," he replied, his tone laced with impatience, as though the weight of her words was too heavy for him to carry. "You always do this. It's not as bad as you're making it out to be."

RoKo's heart sank, his dismissive words slicing through the fragile hope she had clung to all evening. She took a breath, trying to steady herself. "I'm not overreacting, AV. These feelings—they're real, and I'm scared. If I don't deal with them, I'm afraid everything might spiral out of control."

AV sighed, pushing his plate aside with a careless wave of his hand, as if her emotions were nothing more than an inconvenience. "You're being dramatic, RoKo. Everyone has stress. You just need to toughen up and stop worrying so much."

His words hit her like a slap. RoKo stared at him, searching for any sign of understanding, but all she found was cold impatience. It was like trying to reach someone through thick fog, only to realize they were already too far away to hear you.

She lowered her gaze, feeling the heavy weight of the realization settling in her chest. He simply can't—or won't—see things from my perspective, she thought, the truth of it tightening around her like a vice.

"You know," she murmured, almost to herself, her voice barely above a whisper, "I can't keep doing this."

But AV barely reacted, already moving on in his mind, as if her words hadn't even registered. To him, this was just another conversation to brush off. But for RoKo, it was a turning point. A moment of clarity that cut through the fog of her confusion.

As RoKo let her thoughts settle, she began to see the quiet beauty in what had unfolded. The truth hit her like a soft wave—life wasn't about getting even or seeking justice for every hurt. It wasn't about making someone pay. People entered our lives for a reason, and sometimes that reason was simply to help us learn more about ourselves.

She realized there was no lesson she needed to teach AV, no revenge that would bring her peace. Her energy, she decided, was too precious to waste on anger or trying to make him see her side of things. That wasn't her job anymore. The struggle to change oneself was hard enough; why waste her energy trying to change someone else? Her focus had shifted—away from him, away from their fractured story—towards healing, towards moving forward.

With a slow, deliberate exhale, RoKo released the weight that had been pressing down on her chest, that crushing need to be understood.

There was a strange peace in accepting what she couldn't control, a quiet freedom in letting go of the anger she had held onto for so long. AV would find his own path to understanding, or maybe he wouldn't. That wasn't for her to decide.

RoKo knew now where her energy belonged. It wasn't meant for him, or for anyone else who failed to see her clearly. Her energy was hers, meant for her own growth, her own path forward. Every moment spent on AV, every attempt to control his perception, had been draining her—slowly, invisibly.

And by now the initial wave of pain had begun to ebb, something else slowly emerging—a simmering anger that crept up quietly, demanding her attention. It wasn't just anger at AV for his dismissiveness; it was anger at herself. How had she, someone who always prided herself on her strength and independence, allowed herself to get to this point?

She replayed the past months in her mind, the small compromises, the subtle concessions that had slowly chipped away at her sense of self. She had given so much power to someone who, in hindsight, had never truly deserved it. The realization hit her like a cold, hard slap: she had reduced herself to begging for validation from a man who had never seen her for who she truly was. The sting of that truth cut deeper than any words he had ever spoken.

Why? she wondered. Why had she lost herself so completely in AV? What was it about him that had made her forget her own worth? Was it the way he had initially made her feel seen, understood in fleeting moments? Or was it something deeper, something within herself she had hoped he could fill?

The more she unraveled it, the clearer it became—the love she had sought from AV was the love she had been withholding from herself. It was a sobering, but powerful realization.

The anger that had simmered began to fade, replaced by a steady, determined resolve. RoKo realized that as painful as AV's departure was, it might actually be a blessing in disguise. Yes, he had misunderstood her, judged her unfairly, but maybe this was exactly what she needed to finally see the truth. *The truth that she had been holding on to something that was never really hers, trying to mend something that had already been broken.*

She refused to let this breakup break her. Instead, she would use it as a spark—a spark to ignite her own growth, fuel to rebuild herself, and rediscover the strength that had always been within her, waiting to be unleashed. She would rise from this, stronger and more confident than ever.

As she looked back on the relationship, the clarity of hindsight illuminated what she hadn't wanted to admit before: *AV had never truly seen her. He had never really understood her. He had only seen a version of her that conveniently fit into his own story, his own expectations and needs. He had crafted his own narrative of who RoKo was—a version that suited him, but wasn't her reality.*

And it never would be.

AV had been more invested in his own narrative than in truly knowing her. RoKo had been cast in his story, playing a role that fit his expectations, but he had never taken the time to understand the real her.

As she looked ahead, RoKo knew the road wouldn't be easy. There would be challenges, countless moments of doubt, and flashes of heartache that would come uninvited.

She was ready. Ready to leave behind the pain of the past, ready to embrace the new possibilities ahead.

RoKo had also learned an important truth: there's a difference between how you feel about someone and how they make you feel. Her feelings for AV had been real, no doubt about that, but she couldn't ignore the way his actions had chipped away at her. While she had seen him as charismatic, intelligent, fun—his presence had left her feeling lonely, stressed, and constantly questioning her own value.

That realization was crucial. No matter how extraordinary someone may seem, if they consistently make you feel insignificant, that's your reality.

RoKo took a deep breath, closing her eyes for a moment, and when she opened them again, a renewed sense of determination filled her. She was ready to write the next chapter of her life—a chapter where her worth was defined by her, not by how someone else made her feel.

As she reflected on her journey, a passage from *The Alchemist* by Paulo Coelho came to mind—a book one of her former bosses had gifted her. Maybe it was time to re-read it, to rediscover the lessons within. The passage echoed in her mind:

"When you pray to catch the bus, you don't just whisper a wish and casually stroll down the street—you sprint like your life depends on it. You pray with all your heart, and then you run with all your might. Because if you give it everything you've got and still miss the bus, it wasn't meant for you. But if you don't run, if you don't pour your soul into that chase, you'll always wonder if that bus was supposed to be yours."

RoKo knew this all too well. She had given it everything—the love, the effort, the faith. And still, it wasn't meant for her. But that was okay. She believed deeply that rejection wasn't failure—it was just life's way of saying, *"This isn't for you right now."*

And with that, RoKo took a deep, cleansing breath, standing tall, her heart lighter. She was ready to face whatever came next, knowing that she was stronger, more resilient, and more determined than she had ever been before.

SEVEN
THE HEART ACHE!!!

If only life were as straightforward as the promises we make to ourselves when we're hurting. In those moments of raw emotion, everything feels so clear, shaped by the overwhelming force of pain and anger. You vow to be stronger, wiser, and more guarded, convinced that these promises will shield you from future hurt. Yet, life's twists and turns often break these vows, proving that our resolves are fragile against the relentless unpredictability of life.

Heartbreak feels like being caught in a storm—chaotic, overwhelming, and disorienting. The sharp pain and anger drive you to make bold promises, believing they'll be your lifeline amid the turmoil. However, as the storm subsides, these promises prove to be mere bandages, offering temporary relief but no permanent cure. Eventually, you're left exposed, confronting the raw truth that healing is far more complex than you had hoped.

That's the reality—resolves made in the heat of the moment often don't stand the test of time. And so it was with RoKo. She had made a strong resolve the day before, determined to move on, to rebuild herself. But as she woke up the next morning, her eyes still heavy from the tears she cried herself to sleep with, that resolve began to waver. The numbness from the night before had given way to a dull, throbbing pain that wrapped around her chest like a vice. *It wasn't just heartache—it was grief, a grief that clung to her like a shadow, the grief of a relationship that had died but refused to let go, suffocating her with its quiet persistence.*

Grief is a living thing. It doesn't follow a schedule; it doesn't abide by rules or logic. It arrives uninvited, at the most inconvenient times, and stays as long as it pleases. RoKo, desperate to escape it, tried everything—working herself to exhaustion, drowning her sorrows in another night of drinking, burying herself under a mountain of tasks. But grief is patient. It waits for you to finish, then comes back, stronger, bolder, refusing to be ignored, refusing to be silenced.

When it shows up—however it shows up—you have to let it in. You have to sit with it, let it seep into your bones, and ride the wave until it finally begins to ebb. RoKo was learning this the hard way. She was learning that you cannot rush through grief any more than you can rush through love. One can rush through fleeting infatuations, but not love. *Both love and grief demand to be felt, to be experienced fully, to be embraced in all their messy, overwhelming intensity.*

The conversation with AV haunted her, each word echoing in her mind, refusing to fade. Her heart was shattered, she was in pain, and she was engulfed in grief so deep it felt like it might never end. And she knew that healing would take time, that it would be a slow and painful process, but it was the only way forward. Because that's how you heal. That's how you grow. And that's how you become whole again. But the strength she so desperately wanted to summon felt just out of reach, like a distant star flickering on the horizon—visible, yet unattainable.

The strength felt just out of reach. No matter how hard she tried to pull herself together, she couldn't shake the impact of AV's words. They had left her in a state of shock and trauma: *"This is who you are!" Those words cut deeper than any physical wound, reverberating through her mind like a cruel mantra. She couldn't stop hearing them, couldn't stop wondering what he had truly meant. How could he reduce her to such a simplistic and hurtful label? What did he mean, "This is who you are"?*

The pain of being unjustly blamed for something she hadn't done was almost too much to bear. It felt as though AV had cast her as the villain in their story, making her feel as if she had committed some unforgivable crime. His words made her feel dirty, as if she had betrayed him in the worst possible way, like he had walked in on her with another man. This wasn't just hurtful—it was devastating. *She had thought about ending things before, had even imagined saying goodbye, knowing in her heart that their relationship was fragile and might not last. But this—this wasn't how it was supposed to end. Not with accusations, not with blame, not with such a harsh and final dismissal.*

She found herself questioning everything: Was it her ego that was bruised, that part of her that screamed, *"How could he leave me?"* Or was it something deeper, something more integral to who she was? Was it her self-respect that had been trampled, crushed under the weight of AV's harsh judgment? The lines between pride and dignity blurred in her mind, leaving her in a state of painful, unresolved turmoil. *She couldn't tell where one ended and the other began.*

All she knew was that she felt broken in ways she hadn't thought possible. RoKo's mind raced, trying to piece together the fragments of her shattered self, trying to understand how she had ended up here. The love she had given, the trust she had placed in AV, now felt like a betrayal of her own values. She had given him everything—her heart and her soul—and in return, he had torn her down with a few simple words. But she wasn't ready to let those words define her.

She knew she had to find a way to reclaim herself, to rebuild the person she was before AV's judgment had left her questioning everything.

To AV, the relationship no longer felt like love but a heavy anchor pulling him deeper into waters he didn't want to swim in. What had once been a source of light and excitement now suffocated him, like a flame slowly starved of oxygen. The spark that had once set his world alight had fizzled, leaving behind only a stifling sense of obligation. RoKo's needs, which had once felt natural to fulfill, now loomed over him like a mountain he couldn't climb. Every request, every emotional demand felt like one more stone added to his already heavy load, and he found himself offering her only scraps of affection, never enough to satisfy either of them. Each gesture felt forced, each moment with her another drop from his already empty well, leaving him emotionally parched and drained.

The idea of ending the relationship felt like the first breath after being submerged underwater for too long. It wasn't just about peace of mind—it was about reclaiming the space he desperately needed, the autonomy he had lost in the tidal wave of expectations. He wanted to break free from the guilt that weighed heavily on him, the constant reminder that he was always falling short, never enough for RoKo's ever-growing needs. What they once had—the laughter, the connection—had faded into routine, an echo of something that used to be.

Work had become his refuge, the adrenaline of new challenges and the rush of travel reigniting the sense of purpose and excitement he had once found in RoKo. The dopamine hits he now craved came not from their time together, but from the world outside their relationship. The love that had once been a source of joy now felt like a distant memory, blurred by the pressures of reality, and AV was ready—aching, even—to leave it behind and reclaim his life.

But for RoKo, this breakup was something entirely different. It wasn't just the end of a relationship; it was the destruction of everything she had built her identity around. Her sense of self had become so entwined with him that losing him felt like losing herself. The thought of him walking away, of never hearing his voice again, shattered her to the core. It wasn't just about losing a partner; it was about losing the person she had become with him. The very idea of it left her feeling hollow, as if her individuality, her very essence, was slipping away with him.

She could feel the cold grip of fear tightening around her heart, the fear of facing a life without him, a life where she would have to redefine who she was all over again.But as the relationship dragged on, she realized that AV had already made his choice. He was already halfway out the door, leaving her behind to pick up the pieces of a life she no longer recognized. And in that moment, RoKo knew—this was the end, not just of their relationship, but of the person she had been with him. She would have to rebuild, reimagine, and rediscover herself, piece by painful piece.

A week later, RoKo picked up the phone and called AV. No answer. She tried again, but the silence on the other end was deafening, a void that seemed to echo back her own despair. Desperation clawed at her as she poured her heart into a long, heartfelt text. She apologized profusely, her fingers trembling as she typed, asking him to talk, to sort things out. *She reminded him of their pact—the promise they had made to each other. When the time came to say goodbye, they had vowed to do it with grace and maturity. They had agreed to meet, to hug, to kiss, and to part as mature adults, not as strangers.*

But AV didn't respond. The silence from him was like a cold, unyielding wall, each passing hour intensifying the ache in her chest. It was as if her words had been swallowed by the void, right into a black hole, leaving RoKo feeling more alone than ever. She knew, with a painful finality, that there was nothing more she could do. She had laid everything out before him, her heart raw and exposed, and now it was his choice whether to respond or not.

The options swirled in her mind—she could have gone to his city, like she had so many times before, walked right into his office where she was no stranger, and confronted him face to face. She could have stormed into his life one last time, demanding the closure she so desperately needed. But as those thoughts badgered her, she made a conscious choice to hold onto her sanity and maturity. She knew deep down that doing something drastic wouldn't change the outcome; it would only compromise her own self-respect.

She chose to stay silent, even though it felt like swallowing broken glass, each moment hurting more. But in that silence, she found a small strength, a way to protect what was left of her. The pain in her heart grew sharper, but she believed it was the only way to keep her sense of self. The silence stretched between them like a gap that couldn't be fixed, holding all the heartbreak, the unshed tears, and the love that had nowhere else to go.

And she wrote him a mental letter:

Armaan,

I loved you with all my heart and always will. It's incredibly hard to live knowing that you feel hatred toward me, a feeling so clear in your heart and your eyes. I know I made a mistake—picking up that bottle of wine was something I should have resisted. I was weak, vulnerable, and I failed—miserably.

All I want is to collapse into your embrace one last time, dig in and cry my heart out, even if it means it would truly be the last time.

Moving away and trying to move on has been anything but easy.

I remember you saying I'd forget it all and move on in two days—well, these have been the longest two days of my life, each moment dragging endlessly.

I know I have to deal with this on my own, and there's no other way out. But believe me, I feel the weight of this pain every single day. I just hope that one day—maybe not today, but someday—I'll be able to move on.

You know I love you and always will, because that's who RoKo is, and who she always will be.

For RoKo it is. Aabh RoKo ko kaun rokega :)

EIGHT

SOMETHING THAT CHANGED THE SHAPE OF THEIR HEART'S...

RoKo immersed herself in her work, determined to keep up a strong, happy face despite the pain clawing at her from within. She threw herself into her workout routines, pushing her body to the limit. She was walking 10 kilometers a day, along with hitting the gym every day. Was it out of spite, a way to release her pain, or just an attempt at a revenge body? She would laugh at herself sometimes, but in those moments, she didn't dwell on it much—she just needed some kind of relief.

Her walks turned into long, internal dialogues with AV, where she tried to make sense of what had happened and offered him all the justifications she could muster in her mind. Each step felt like a conversation, each breath a plea for understanding. She rehearsed the words she wished she had said, replayed his cold responses, and tried, over and over, to find some peace in the chaos that had become her life.

Desperate for some kind of peace, RoKo sought out therapists, working tirelessly on herself because the pain was unbearable, and the stigma seemed impossible to shake—it ran deep, deeply rooted in her very being. She felt dirty every moment, even though logically she knew that if someone called her a monkey, it didn't make her one. But here, in her mind, she was deeply tied to AV, and when he said, *'This is who you are,' it felt like a punch to the gut, crushing her self-respect. Those words echoed in her mind, like a cruel mantra she couldn't escape.*

Within four to five weeks, something unsettling began to shift in her health. Instead of improving, her heart rate dropped alarmingly low. Each morning, her Apple Watch would ping with notifications, alerting her to the concerning numbers as soon as she woke up. This relationship had impacted her more than she ever imagined—it was far more than just a fling. A month later, she texted AV again, requesting for a closure because the pain was becoming unbearable. Her health was taking a toll with each passing day, and then, just the next day, she suffered a minor cardiac arrest. She didn't die—she had a lot more to do in life—but the incident was a serious wake-up call. The grief that had wrapped around her heart had manifested physically, nearly taking her life.

However, she chose not to inform AV, for she knew he would, in his mind, feel it was RoKo's trick trying to get his attention. It wasn't about drawing his sympathy, and deep down, she feared that if he knew and still didn't care, it would break her even more. The fear of rejection kept her silent, and life moved on.

Fast forward another five weeks, and it was the last day of her business unit before shutting down for good. She was devastated, having lost everything—her business, her identity, her so-called love, and the team she had so proudly and meticulously built.

Something deep inside her stirred—a familiar pull reminding her that AV had once walked this painful path with her. Almost instinctively, she reached for her phone and dialed his number around 11 a.m., hoping this time would be different. But as usual, there was no answer, just silence.

The only thing louder than the quiet on the other end was the flutter of her butterflies—her inner voice, restless and relentless. "What are you doing?" they practically screamed at her. "Why are you calling him again? Isn't the rejection enough? The humiliation? Why are you chasing more?"

The butterflies fluttered furiously, warning her, mocking her for still holding on. But amidst their frantic questions, the wisest one remained silent, sensing her pain and knowing now wasn't the time to push—just to understand.

In her despair, she turned to a bottle once again. The familiar burn of alcohol provided a fleeting sense of comfort, a way to quiet the overwhelming grief threatening to consume her. Sitting alone in a posh, upscale pub, she let the drinks wash over her, sinking deeper into a haze of intoxication.

Just as she thought she had silenced the world around her, her phone rang. It was AV, calling her back after her unanswered call that morning.

She answered, her voice heavy with emotion, the words spilling out in a raw, unfiltered way. She shared how lost she felt, how stuck she had become, unable to move forward or leave the past behind. The frustration and hurt in her voice were clear, as she asked for one last conversation, some sense of closure—something to finally make sense of it all.

But AV, firm and distant, said no. He insisted that meeting again would only bring more pain, that it would make things worse for both of them. "It's over," he said. And though his words cut deep, a part of her knew he was right. Seeing him would only make her miss him more, reigniting feelings she was struggling to bury. This was the final chapter, and she had to find a way to close it on her own terms.

RoKo, her voice trembling, asked, "Can we atleast talk once in a while?" AV retorted sharply, *"For What, can you at the very least just please let me have some peace? I'm still scared every time I see your name pop up on my phone. I just want to be free, to not feel this fear anymore."*

This was the second crushing blow AV delivered to her. Even in her drunken state, RoKo realized it was time to hang up and never call again. She ended the call and, on her way back home, sent AV a flurry of regrettable messages—threats she didn't mean, fuelled by her pain and drunken mindlessness. Each word was a cry for help, a desperate attempt to make him feel the hurt she was drowning in. The next morning, she felt awful about what she had done, but she knew it was over. There was no point in dropping an apology text, and she resolved never to call him again.

The realization hit her like a tidal wave—there was nothing left to say, nothing left to salvage. She had given everything, and all that remained was the painful emptiness of letting go. As she sat in the stillness of her room, surrounded by the remnants of what once was, *RoKo finally understood that the closure she sought could only come from within. She would have to find a way to heal, to rebuild, without AV. The chapter had ended, and though the pages were stained with tears, it was time to start a new one—one that was written solely by her.*

Days turned into weeks, and weeks into months. RoKo clung to her resolve, though it was anything but easy. Each day felt like a battle, and though she had resolved to move on, she found herself talking to AV in her mind for hours, imagining what they could have been. The conversations were vivid, as if he were right there beside her, and for those brief moments, the pain of his absence softened.

Then, out of the blue, three months later, as she finished her post-dinner stroll, her phone buzzed with a message. It wasn't from a name but a number she knew all too well—AV. Her heart skipped a beat as she stared at the screen, disbelieving. The message read, "Rite," his usual response whenever RoKo said, "I love you.", AV would reply saying Ritee!! That's all he could manage. She froze, a mix of disbelief and joy flooding her senses. Her heart raced, and butterflies filled her stomach, just like every time she was about to meet AV. For a fleeting moment, everything felt right again, as if the past months had been nothing more than a bad dream.

But then the timing struck her as odd. It was 10:10 p.m., well beyond the limits they had agreed on for texting each other. She thought maybe he was drinking with friends. Her mind warned her to tread carefully, but her heart, ever hopeful, urged her to respond. She typed back, "Right." Almost immediately, he replied, "Delhi" She answered, "No, Hyderabad," and then sent another message: "You?" His reply was simple but loaded with possibilities: "Delhi till Friday."

Now, RoKo knew that for the next few days, she had an open line to him—he had opened that door by letting her know he was traveling. She felt a surge of excitement, the familiar longing rising within her. She wanted to fly out the next day, to be near him, to find any excuse to see him, but she held herself back. That night, another sleepless one, she lay awake, torn between hope and caution. Why had he texted her? It was supposed to be over—he could have just let it be. And now, she found herself wondering if maybe AV was right; maybe meeting would only make things worse.

But she was still madly in love with AV, and despite all her efforts, she hadn't yet been able to let him go. The thought of him still stirred something deep within her, something she couldn't simply turn off. It had been precisely six months since their last contact when she found herself, almost against her will, texting him once again.

"Can we catch up for coffee?" she typed, her fingers trembling slightly. She hesitated, feeling the weight of every word, knowing how much was riding on this message. "*I know you would never ask—I clearly remember, you never said you wanted to meet. However, whenever I told you I was traveling, you always made time for me, spending as many hours as you could with me. So, I realized I need to ask you this, and that's what I'm doing. You know I loved you, I still do, and I always will, whether you believe it or not.*" She paused, her heart pounding, before she finally hit send. After a moment, she continued, "Please, let's just talk. I need closure."

AV's reply was almost immediate, but it wasn't what she had expected. "Can you stop writing all these things in text messages, please, and move to Telegram?" Her heart sank as she read the words. Telegram had been their mode of communication, a place she had deleted to try and forget him. But now, she felt a flicker of hope—he wanted to talk.

Quickly, almost frantically, she reinstalled Telegram, her hands shaking as she logged back in. She texted him again, "I'll be in your city on the 11th for work. It would mean a lot if we could meet." Her breath caught as she waited for his response. His reply was simple: "Yes."

A flood of relief washed over her. Finally, she thought, she would get the closure she desperately needed. The painful nights and days she had endured now had a purpose, a light at the end of the tunnel. The prospect of seeing him one last time gave her something to hold onto. She clung to that hope, ignoring the small voice in the back of her mind that warned her it might not go as she wished. This was no work trip, it was personal—she had planned this visit solely to see him, making it a four-day trip just in case things worked out between them and she could spend more time with him.

The days leading up to the trip were a blur of anticipation and anxiety. RoKo rehearsed what she would say, imagining every possible scenario, trying to prepare herself for whatever might come. But deep down, she knew that no amount of preparation could shield her from the reality of seeing AV again. Still, she hoped—hoped that this meeting would bring the closure she so desperately sought, or perhaps, something more.

But after that, the line went dead again—no messages, no calls, nothing. And this was nothing new. In the highs of love, RoKo never realized that AV hardly ever called her first; he always responded to her calls—some right away, but most after a couple of hours. It was like chasing the dopamine rush gamblers feel, pulling the lever on a slot machine, hoping each spin would finally hit the jackpot. How naïve she had been!

On the 11th, they were supposed to meet at 6 p.m. By 4 p.m., a message appeared on her phone: "Did you land?" It was from AV, a simple question, but it carried the weight of all her hopes. She replied affirmatively, trying to keep her excitement in check, though her heart was racing. This could be the moment she had been waiting for—the moment they might finally talk, really talk.

RoKo got ready with meticulous care, choosing an outfit that reflected the woman she wanted him to see: confident, composed, and still alluring. She had lost weight over the past few months—not from the gym, but from sleepless nights and heartbreak—but she still looked good. She had become a master at masking her emotions, at hiding the turmoil that churned beneath the surface.

She arrived at their usual spot by 6 p.m., her heart pounding with anticipation. But AV wasn't there. Her eyes darted around the room, scanning every face, every shadow, hoping to catch a glimpse of him. The minutes ticked by—6:30, then 7:00. Each passing minute felt like a year, stretching out the uncertainty, the doubt.

Finally, at 8:05 p.m., AV walked in, but not to their usual bar at the hotel—he had chosen a different restaurant in the hotel this time. RoKo caught a glimpse of him from the corner of her eye while she was on a video call. Her heart lurched as she quickly wrapped up the call, her hands trembling slightly. She hurried over to his table, trying to compose herself, but her emotions were teetering on the edge.

RoKo was already three drinks in as she waited, carefully masking the buzz that had begun to settle over her. The alcohol gave her a veneer of calm, but beneath that surface, her thoughts churned in chaos. "What would you like to have?" she asked him, her voice steady despite the storm raging inside her.

"Lime water," he replied. She raised an eyebrow. *"Seriously?"* she thought, unable to hide her surprise. "Yes," he said, then added, "I only have 15 minutes. Mom's not well, and I need to get back."

Her mind screamed in protest—*What the fuck, breadcrumbs again? Are you fucking out of your mind, RoKo? How can you stoop so low for this guy, even if he's the only one in the world?* But she kept her composure. She swallowed her pride, trying to mask the hurt that was bubbling up inside her. They exchanged couple of words, and RoKo, despite being lost in his presence, asked about the big project he had been working on. They had once planned to celebrate its success with a trip to the Maldives. "Not yet closed," he said, his tone flat, almost indifferent.

She nodded, her mind struggling to process the reality of the moment. She hardly knew what she was saying, too overwhelmed by just being near him again. The anticipation that had built up over weeks now felt misplaced, foolish even. Then, just as suddenly as he had arrived, he stood up. "I have to go," he said, his voice cool, distant.

RoKo nodded, trying to hide her tears. This wasn't closure; this was a slap in the face yet again. But he was already gone, leaving her alone with the echoes of their brief exchange.

The pain was too much to bear, too raw, too real. She headed straight to the bar where her reserved spot awaited. One drink led to another, then another, until she lost count. Each sip was an attempt to drown out the ache, to silence the relentless voice in her head that kept asking, *why?* Why him? Why can't you let go? The questions echoed with every swallow, but no answer ever came. Drunk and desperate, she went to a club, trying to dance away the pain. But even in the throbbing beat of the music, she couldn't escape him.

Her thoughts spiralled—*If it's meant to be, he'll come back. He'll knock on my door again or text me.* And as if the universe was mocking her, AV texted: "Will meet you on Friday."

She gave herself a high five, feeling a rush of relief. Finally, her persistence had paid off, or so she thought. She wanted to sing the song Baarish lete aana by Darshan Raval out loud to him for old times' sake:

Aatey ho toh baarish lete aana, Jee bhar ke rone ka dil karta hai.

Waqt ki thi humse kuch naraazgi, Keh na sake hum woh baatein aaj bhi. Jinko liye, hum tum ho gaye judaa.

She spent the next two days in her hotel room, looking at his office from the terrace. That's why this hotel was her favorite—it made her feel close to him, even when he wasn't there. She remembered how, in the past, she had danced on that terrace, and he had smiled down at her from his office, amused by her craziness.

But little did she know, he wasn't in the office those two days for he was travelling out of Chennai. He hadn't been watching her; he hadn't even been thinking of her. The realization, when it came, would hit her like a ton of bricks, leaving her to wonder how long she could keep up this charade, pretending that everything was fine when, in truth, she was falling apart.

Friday came, and they were supposed to meet at 6 p.m. RoKo sat at their usual table, her heart fluttering again with both anticipation and dread. The minutes ticked by slowly, each one amplifying the silence between them. Then, at 6:05 p.m., AV walked straight to her table without hesitation, as if this time he knew exactly where she would be. Such was their chemistry, an unspoken connection that had once made her feel special, but now felt like a bittersweet echo of what they had lost.

She smiled brightly, though her heart thudded heavily in her chest, a mix of nerves and hope. Their greeting was subdued, almost formal, without so much as a handshake, let alone a hug. It was as if the invisible wall that had been growing between them had finally solidified, keeping them at a careful distance. She offered him a beer, trying to break the tension, but he declined. Undeterred, she ordered one for herself, hoping he wouldn't mind. He ordered a coffee instead, the choice starkly contrasting the vibrant memories of their past, where they had shared drink after drink, their laughter and conversations fuelled by alcohol.

After a few pleasantries, he told her he only had an hour—he had a dinner meeting after. *Seriously?* RoKo thought, but said nothing. It wasn't as bad as the 15 minutes he had offered last time, she reasoned—at least it was something. The resignation in her thoughts mirrored the dwindling hopes she had clung to for so long.

He asked about her, and she tried to explain how she was still stuck, despite therapy, despite working out, despite everything.

But his response was dismissive, saying she was being dramatic again. This time, though, the blow was softer, more resigned. She ordered another drink, offered him a beer again, and he finally agreed, saying he had been off alcohol for 2.5 months but would make an exception. *"Maybe the last one ever together,"* he said, and they clinked glasses with a sense of finality that was hard to ignore. For a moment, the memory of their first drink together flashed before RoKo's eyes—their first meeting in that room, where everything had felt so full of possibility. From that moment to where they stood now, so close physically yet so distant in their hearts, the contrast was stark and heartbreaking.

As the conversation meandered, AV pointed out that her biggest mistake had been picking up that bottle of wine and her phone that fateful night. RoKo knew better than to delve into that painful memory—both of them were too raw, too hurt to go there again. They knew it was over between them, even if RoKo had hoped otherwise. She listened as he shared his successes, genuinely happy for him, but couldn't help but feel the weight of her own sadness, still stuck at the lowest point in her life.

Time flew by, as it often does when alcohol is involved, and just like their 11 months and 11 days together, where they had been drunk 80% of the time, the moments slipped away. They had shared so much, but it was always under the influence, always tinged with the haze of alcohol. It was as if the clarity they needed to see each other clearly had always been just out of reach, hidden beneath the veneer of intoxication.

At 8 p.m., AV stood up and said he had to leave. RoKo, feeling the moment slipping away like sand through her fingers, asked if he could stay for just another 15 minutes. But he shook his head, a firm "no," leaving her with no choice but to accept it. She told herself to stay strong, but the disappointment weighed heavily on her, a sinking feeling that this was really the end.

Before letting him go, her heart screamed to ask him—Why? Why did you do that to me? How could you hide such an important part of your life from me? The words almost reached her lips, but she swallowed them down. She wanted to demand answers, to know who he was protecting—himself or her. Had you just told me, maybe things would've been different, she thought, her mind spinning with the possibilities. But she knew the truth, no matter how painful. It wouldn't have changed a thing. AV believed she was to blame, and even if she revealed that she knew about his secret, nothing would heal the damage already done.

So, in one final act of love, she sacrificed her own need for closure to protect him from the guilt. She let him live in his version of the story, believing that he had spared her the truth, thinking it made him noble. Only she was left hurting, carrying the weight of what she knew. But still, she just let it go. She let him go, choosing his peace over her own.

They walked out of the restaurant together, the air between them thick yet again with unspoken words, with everything they wanted to say but couldn't. As they reached the street, AV mentioned that Ranga was driving him and that he didn't want to be seen with anyone. RoKo understood, though the sting of his distance felt sharper now. She asked for a hug, something to hold onto in this moment of finality, hoping it might give her a sense of closure.

AV obliged, but only with a side hug, offering just a sliver of the comfort she desperately craved. He kissed her on the head, a gesture that should have been tender, but felt hollow in its simplicity. "You know I care for you. Stay strong and do good," he told her, his words kind, but distant. RoKo knew this was just the beer talking—otherwise, he might never have said those words. But it didn't matter. This was the end—the final, irrevocable end of their story.

As he walked away, disappearing into the night, RoKo stood there, feeling the cold night air on her skin, the emptiness settling in her heart. It was over, not with a bang, but with a quiet, almost anticlimactic end. She had hoped for closure, for something to hold onto, but all she was left with was the stark reality that he was gone, and she was alone.

Their story began with such promise, a world woven with joy, laughter, and a bond that felt unbreakable. In those early days, RoKo and AV believed they were invincible. Every conversation, every shared glance, carried the weight of something special, something that felt like it could last forever. They created a private universe where nothing could go wrong, where the connection between them was so strong that it seemed impossible to imagine anything that could come between them. It was a time of hope, of endless possibilities, where they felt that their love (no, her love and his CARE) could withstand any challenge that life might throw their way.

But as time wore on, the vibrant connection they once shared began to dim. The once effortless conversations turned strained, punctuated by silences that grew heavier with each passing day. AV, who had always been so present, so engaged, started to pull away, retreating into a space that RoKo couldn't reach. The warmth that had once characterized their relationship was replaced by a cold distance that neither of them wanted to acknowledge, but both could feel. *It wasn't that AV didn't care—perhaps he cared too much, but he was lost, unable to articulate the growing disinterest that gnawed at him. Maybe he feared confrontation, or maybe he didn't want to hurt RoKo, but in trying to protect her, he only deepened the divide between them. His emotions became a maze with no clear exit, and RoKo found herself wandering through it, lost and confused, unable to find her way back to the connection they once shared.*

RoKo could sense the change, and it tore at her. Every attempt she made to bridge the gap, to voice her fears, felt like pushing against a wall that wouldn't budge. She clung to the hope that things could return to the way they were, that the love they had could be rekindled, but deep down, she knew they were drifting apart. The words they needed to say—the ones that might have saved them—remained unspoken, locked behind walls of fear and pride. And as the days turned into weeks, the gap between them widened, an unspoken barrier that neither had the courage to cross.

Their relationship became a delicate dance of avoidance, a performance where both partners moved carefully around the issues that lay between them, never daring to confront the truth that could have set them free. AV couldn't bring himself to admit that his heart was no longer in it, and RoKo couldn't muster the strength to demand the honesty she desperately needed. *They continued in this painful limbo, each hoping for change but unwilling to be the one to initiate it. The silence between them grew deafening, each unspoken word building the wall higher, making it harder to see the other clearly.*

Then came the final, devastating blow—a misunderstanding that spiralled out of control, fuelled by fear and insecurity. AV, overwhelmed by his own unresolved emotions, accused RoKo of a betrayal that existed only in his mind. The accusation was like a dagger to RoKo's heart, a wound that cut so deep it left her reeling, her world turned upside down. *In that moment, everything they had built together crumbled, their love now overshadowed by doubt and regret.* The trust that had once been so strong was shattered, and with it, the foundation of their relationship.

And so, their story reached its inevitable, heartbreaking conclusion. What began with so much potential, with a love that seemed capable of enduring anything, ended not with a dramatic farewell, but with a quiet, devastating whimper. RoKo was left to pick up the pieces of her shattered heart, while AV walked away, burdened by the guilt of what could never be undone. Both were left wondering what might have been, haunted by the question of what could have happened if they had only found the strength to speak their truth, to face their fears together. The story of RoKo and AV, once filled with so much promise, ended as a tale of missed opportunities, of love lost to silence and unspoken words.

In the end, it wasn't a dramatic event that tore them apart—it was the silence. *The silence of unspoken fears, of doubts that festered without being addressed, of love that was slowly choked by a lack of communication.* As she walked back to her room, Matt Hansen's song played in the background, perfectly capturing the moment.

Sometimes you need the rain. To know you miss the sun
Sometimes you need the pain. To know it isn't love
Sometimes the one you hold. You gotta let 'em go, you gotta let 'em go

AV walked away, carrying the weight of his own perceptions, his heart heavy with regret. He knew, deep down, that he had failed—not just RoKo, but himself. He had let his insecurities take control, allowing them to drive a wedge between them, and now all that remained was the haunting question of what might have been. He replayed their final moments together, the words he wished he had said, the feelings he wished he had shared. He had let fear dictate his actions, and now, all he was left with was the hollow ache of a love that slipped through his fingers.

As the days turned into weeks, both RoKo and AV found themselves struggling to move on. RoKo threw herself into work, into her routines once again, trying to distract herself from the gnawing emptiness that AV had left behind. But no matter how busy she kept herself, she couldn't escape the thoughts of him that lingered in the back of her mind. She wondered if he thought of her too, if he regretted how things ended, but she knew that even if he did, it wouldn't change anything. *The damage was done, and some things, once broken, can never be mended.*

AV, too, found it hard to convince himself that he had made the right decision. He tried to rationalize it, telling himself that it was better this way, that they were better off apart. But the guilt and regret clung to him like a shadow, a constant reminder of the love he had lost. He knew that he had let go of something precious, something that he might never find again, and that realization ate away at him, refusing to be silenced

In the end, theirs was a story of two people who once meant the world to each other slowly drifted apart. Not because they stopped caring, but because they were too afraid to confront the truths that lay between them.

And so, it ended—not with a dramatic farewell, but with a quiet, painful acceptance that there was no longer a "THEY." The love that had once felt so certain was now just a memory, a "WHAT IF" that would linger in their hearts long after they had gone their separate ways.

|| And this was for now, In the Moment : The END ||

NINE

CAUGHT IN THE PULL — WHEN MEMORIES RESURFACE

The first month, it consumes you—every waking moment, every breath you take, it's there, haunting you, a shadow that won't let go. You relive it constantly, over and over, as if your mind refuses to let you forget. It doesn't matter what you do or how hard you try to distract yourself, it clings to you like a second skin.

People, well-meaning but clueless, tell you it's part of God's plan. Maybe they're right—maybe there's some grand design behind the pain. But their words do nothing to soothe the ache, and each time someone says it, you have to fight the overwhelming urge to lash out, to scream at them for their blind optimism, to punch them in the face for not understanding that their platitudes are like salt in a wound.

Time trudges on, two or three months pass, and perhaps, just perhaps, you begin to feel something akin to normal. But then, before you know it, two or three years have slipped by, and you find yourself still trying—yeah, damn still trying—to convince yourself that this, too, shall pass—that maybe, just maybe, this wound won't leave a permanent scar. The days start to blend together, the sharp edges of your pain dulling just enough that you can breathe without feeling like your chest is going to cave in.

But then, out of nowhere, it hits you again—a song, a scent, a fleeting moment that transports you back to that day. And suddenly, you're there all over again, the weight of that moment crashing down on you with the same brutal force as before. It's as if no time has passed at all; the pain is fresh, raw, and just as devastating as it was on the day you received the news. *The illusion of healing shatters in an instant, and you're left wondering if this is your new reality—a cycle of moving forward only to be dragged back to the beginning by the ghosts of what once was.*

In those moments, you realize that some scars run deeper than others. They don't fade with time; they become ingrained in your very being, lying just beneath the surface until something, or someone, brings them back to the light. And all you can do is ride the wave, hoping that each time it crashes over you, it will recede just a little bit faster, leaving you a little bit stronger.

For RoKo and AV, this cycle became their existence—a relentless tug-of-war between healing and hurting, between forgetting and remembering. Every time they thought they had moved on, that they were finally free from the grip of the past, something would stir within them—a memory, a fleeting thought, or even just the echo of a shared laugh—and suddenly, they were back at the beginning, caught in the same push and pull. They were bound not just by what they had shared, but by the shadows that lingered long after the light had faded, shadows that neither could fully escape, no matter how far apart they drifted.

Even when they believed they had found peace, that the wounds had finally healed, there was always something— a whisper from the past, a feeling that never quite left—pulling them back into the vortex of their connection. They would find themselves wrestling with emotions they thought were long buried, realizing that *some ties, no matter how much they hurt, can never be completely severed.*

In the quiet moments, when the world slowed down and their thoughts were all they had, they could still feel the connection between them, strong and undeniable. It didn't make sense, but neither distance nor time could erase it. It brought both pain and comfort, yet neither could imagine life without it. They were bound by something deeper than love or loss, something that was simply a part of who they were. And maybe, in some strange way, they always would be.

TEN

THE SILENCE —
SOMETHING THAT AV
LONGED TO, BUT
COULD NEVER SAY!!!

AV missed RoKo just as much as she missed him, but deep down, he knew it wasn't right to reach out, not after everything that had happened. He couldn't bring himself to break her heart again, to reopen wounds that had barely begun to heal. And so, he made the difficult decision to let things remain as they were, to keep his distance even though it pained him.

In the quiet moments, though, his thoughts often drifted back to her. It wasn't just once in a while—it was more frequent than he cared to admit.

RoKo was still a part of him, threaded into the very essence of his life in ways he hadn't fully realized until she was gone. There wasn't a week that passed without her thoughts crossing his mind. She had been an integral part of his days, her presence grounding him from morning till night, especially during his work hours. The rhythm of his day used to flow around her—texts, calls, the comforting knowledge that she was always there, just a message away.

He wanted to say so much more to her, to explain himself, to tell her that he too felt the weight of that morning—the morning that had forever altered the course of their relationship.

The day that drove a wedge between them, a wedge that no amount of regret could remove. And so, in the privacy of his thoughts, in the quiet conversations he had with her in his mind, he penned a message—a message that he wished he could send, but knew he never would. It was as if he were writing her a letter, pouring out everything he couldn't say aloud.

Hey RoKo,

I miss you more than I can express. I wish I could go back and change how I handled that morning, how I let my fear and confusion push you away. You were a part of my life, not just a fleeting moment, but a constant presence that I didn't fully appreciate until it was too late. And you know it well RoKo,

Tujhse duur jo hota hoon, Tukda tukda sota hun, Aankhon mein pirota hoon main raatein.

Tujhse se duur jo hota hoon, Khudko jaise khota hoon, Hothon pe sanjota hu, teri baatein.

I want you to know that I care for you—more than you might ever realize. I didn't want to hurt you, and I never wanted to break your heart. But I see now that by trying to protect you, I ended up causing more pain.

I was scared—scared of what I was feeling, scared of what it meant, and in my fear, I made the wrong choice.

You were my anchor, the person who understood me in ways no one else did. Losing you wasn't just losing a relationship; it was losing a part of myself. I know I can't undo the past, and I don't expect forgiveness. But I need you to know that in my heart, I've never stopped caring for you.

Maybe one day, I'll find the courage to say all of this to you in person. But for now, this is all I can offer—a silent confession, a letter you'll never read, but one that I needed to write.

Please, take care of yourself. You're stronger than you think, and I believe in you, always.

I still wonder and think many a times, telling myself, RoKo rocked my world—both figuratively and in every possible reality. I should have RoKo'ed RoKo.

Goodbye for now, RoKo. But know that in my heart, you'll always have a place.

With all my care,
AV.

[Maybe someday he would find the courage to say all of this to her in person, to bridge the gap that had grown between them. But for now, this was all he could give her—a message from his heart, sent in silence. And in that moment, it was The End.]

And then he wrote another one, maybe this one was the last one and the one which would make it The End

Dear RoKo,

As I sit here, reflecting on everything we've shared, I realize there are some things I need to say—things that I hope will stay with you as you move forward in life.

Growth, RoKo—focus on it. Focus on healing, on becoming the very best and healthiest version of yourself. I know it's not always easy; life has a way of throwing curveballs at us, testing our limits, pushing us to the edge. But it's in those moments, the ones that challenge you the most, that you find out who you really are. And I know you, RoKo—you're stronger than you think.

Turn your attention to your goals and everything you've always wanted to achieve. I remember the countless nights we talked about your dreams, your plans, your visions for the future. You have so much potential, so many ideas bubbling inside you. Make a list of them—make ten if you have to. Write them down, hold them close, and let them guide you.

Distractions, they're everywhere, aren't they? They come in all forms, pulling you away from what truly matters. Bury them, RoKo. Bury those distractions deep and water your intentions. Decide what is and isn't worth your energy, your peace of mind, your time, and your effort. I've seen you pour so much of yourself into things that didn't serve you, that drained you instead of filling you up.

And if it doesn't feel good, RoKo, let it go. I know you're a fighter, someone who holds on when things get tough, but sometimes the bravest thing you can do is let go. Release the things that weigh you down, the things that no longer serve you. Pour your heart and soul into what matters—not to everyone else, but to you. I can't stress that enough. You've spent so much time caring for others, worrying about what they think, trying to meet their expectations. But what about you? What do you want? What sets your soul on fire? Chase that, RoKo. Chase what makes you come alive.

Remember this: What you focus on, whether intentional or not, expands. So focus on the good. Focus on what you already have, on where you want to go. I've always believed that you are capable of having it all, that you are worthy of having it all. And I still do. You deserve a life that's full, a life that's rich with love, with success, with everything you've ever dreamed of.

But remember, it's a journey—day by day, step by step, little by little. Don't rush it. Slow down, breathe, and focus. You've got this, RoKo.You've always had it, even in the moments when you doubted yourself the most.

So, as I say goodbye, know that I'm cheering for you, from wherever I am. Life is waiting for you, RoKo, with all its wonders, all its challenges, and all its possibilities. Embrace it, live it, and don't ever forget how amazing you truly are.

With all the best wishes, Always remember, I Care for you, always did and always will. Rite.

Care and Wishes,
Armaan!!!

ELEVEN

THE UNSPOKEN — WHAT ROKO NEVER HAD THE CHANCE TO SHARE, THOUGH SHE WISHED SHE COULD...

Hey V, Hmmm No, No, No, It's AV, for there is no V left anymore , RITE !!

Every moment we spent together was truly amazing, and I thank you for being a part of my life. I'm sorry we couldn't make more out of it, and I'm sorry for the pain and heartache I caused you. I wish you well, always have and will always do. You will forever be one of the most cherished parts of my life.

*The laughter we shared, the tunes we danced and sang to at the top of our lungs, the Caravan trip, Opa, ZU bar and so, so, so, much more—it was crazy, it was amazing, and it was beyond anything I can put into words. It was truly **Another Level Shit**...ALS*

Now, addressing the elephant in the room—wine. I think I've learned one of the biggest lessons of my life—I don't believe I can handle it anymore. As for you, it's as if you've carved out a permanent space there, a place you seem intent on occupying for quite some time. Years have passed, and I'm still counting, still feeling your presence as strong as ever. I just hope this phase doesn't stretch into twenty years—God forbid! You once told me it would take me two days to move on. Two days, you said with that knowing smile—just two days. But here I am, two days turning into two months, two years... and now I can't help but wonder—did you mean two decades, too? "Because if that's the case, we might have a bit of a situation on our hands. I've got so much more to do, so many places to go, and yeah, I know— it's not your problem, it's mine. And why on earth would you make my problem your problem, But hey, wouldn't that be something? Just a little twist in this story of ours..." And LOL !! I ain't scaring you yet again, You are FREE AV, You are Free, Free, Free!!

When you close the Maldives deal, please share the amazing news—even if it's not through a call or message, at least send it my way telepathically. I'll be the happiest for you, no matter where I am.

You were the sunshine of my life, and I hope you keep shining bright. Thank you for bringing warmth and light into my world as you passed through it. I smile softly, sometimes lost in memories of what we were and who we were together. Those moments still linger in my heart, like a beautiful melody that plays on, even after the song has ended. Just like Tera Chehra Jab Nazar Aaye.

I'm sure we'll meet again, if not in this universe, then maybe in the Metaverse. Even if our paths don't cross in reality, perhaps in some digital world, we'll find each other once more—avatars of who we used to be.

There, we'll create new memories, letting go of the weight of the old ones, and share the moments this universe never allowed us. I can almost see us—our digital selves glowing with the warmth of everything we once were and might still be. If our paths ever cross in that space, it will be a chapter written differently, free of the burdens we carried here.

Cheers! Till we meet again—whether in this universe, the metaverse, or perhaps some other universe.

PS: If we meet again—and I know deep down you feel it too, even if it's hard to say out loud—we'll find each other. Rite? Fir mulakaat hogi kabhi, Tumhe hum yaad aayenge ya nahi !!!

Letter From The Author -

It's Not Goodbye, It's Until We Meet Again!!!

Here we are, at the end of this chapter in my journey—one that began with a simple dream of publishing my first book, Coach?? I Don't Need ONE!!! In it, I explored the world of executive coaching, demystifying its benefits and tackling whether it's just a fad or a genuine tool for growth. While that journey was insightful, my heart has always belonged to storytelling, and that's why this second book feels even closer to who I am and what I love.

Writing fiction has been a lifelong dream, and seeing it come to life on these pages feels truly magical. For so long—for most of our lives, really—we find ourselves trying to make others proud, searching for their approval. I was no different. But then I realized that I needed to be proud of myself first. And now, here I am, fully appreciating this journey. I'm incredibly proud of what I've created, and the emotions behind it are beyond words.

Thank you for choosing to spend your time with one of my most heartfelt creations. I poured my heart and soul into this story, and I hope it resonated with you—perhaps even reflected parts of your own journey. It's often the little misunderstandings and quiet doubts that can change everything. One of my favorite parts of writing this book was creating RoKo—a character full of life, spontaneity, and charm. Her journey was thrilling to write, and I hope you felt that thrill too as you followed along.

I never imagined I'd finish this book so quickly—a few months and 53,666 words later, here we are. Every word, each sentence, each chapter part of a journey filled with emotional highs and lows that not only tested me but also shaped me as a writer.

There were moments of writer's block that felt impossible to break through, times when the story seemed to fall apart—where characters felt disconnected, the plot refused to flow, and words seemed to slip away just when I thought I had found the right ones. It was a constant challenge to dig deeper, to rethink, rewrite, and rediscover the heart of the story. But I kept going, and now, with this chapter behind me, I'm more excited than ever for what's next. In fact, I'm thrilled to share a sneak peek: the next book will reveal the 11 months and 11 days RoKo and AV spent together—a story that I hope you'll find just as captivating.

I'm so grateful that you've walked this path with me. I'd love to hear your reflections—drop me an email at Anjali@avals.in or connect with me on LinkedIn. For now, I handle my accounts personally, and I'd be delighted to hear from you.

This world is smaller than we think, and who knows? Maybe one day our paths will cross—whether it's through a brief smile at an airport, a shared coffee at Starbucks, or an in-depth conversation. Wherever life takes you, in those moments when you're striving to grow stronger, know that I'm silently cheering you on, rooting for you with all my heart. Embrace that Spitfire Energy and dive into this wild adventure we call life.

Wishing you all the abundance, love, and success I hope for in my own journey. Until we meet again, may we all be blessed with growth and new beginnings.

Signing off for now—but the adventure is far from over. Cheers to new stories, new connections, and all that's yet to come. I can't wait to share the next chapter with you.

In Gratitude,
Anjali Vaishal,
The Humble Author.